lovehatelove

from the abstract heart of
robinmichaelsmith

AUTHOR'S NOTE

they (((CIRCLE))) around her
fixed silhouettes on a carousel

riding dark horses

dangling and plunging
dangling and plunging
dangling and plunging

to mad music

FORE

JUNE 8, 2010

This life is an endless quest for truth.

JUNE 9, 2010

Last night a line of storms cut through the area, creating tornadoes, and dropping hail and violent rain. I stood outside under the front archway of my church for several minutes and watched a beautiful arrangement of a dozen cloud-to-ground lightning bolts dash down from the sky. The display was mesmerizing. I finally entered the church when a distant tornado alarm released its mad signal, a warning to the neighborhood's populace that danger was in close proximity.

When I entered the church, darkness buried the congregation and the patrons cowered in the aisles between the pews. I could hear a chant of individual prayers dancing through the place of worship. I felt my way to a random seat, unsure of the location of my husband, who had arrived at the church before me.

Sitting in the unlit house of God with mumbled petitions in the air, children crying, an alarm blasting, and a storm raging, created an air of doom. It was not a passing feeling of dread, but an all-encompassing projection of endless suffering. At that instant of thought, a shock of lightening lit the stained glass of the church and sent a multicolored beam of light across the huge crucifix displayed behind the pulpit. Then the church lights blinked into order, pressing against the congregation's eyes.

Everyone immediately found a seat as I looked for my husband. I located him quickly and went to sit beside him. He grabbed my hand tightly and pushed his shoulder into me, and before he could say a word, my preacher appeared like an apparition and began his sermon without even a cursory mention of the storm.

JUNE 10, 2010

I am heading to Galveston today by way of a spontaneous travel arrangement made by my husband. I have considered Galveston a lustful town of prejudice and greed ever since writing a report about the town when I was in high school.

Galveston's ominous human history began with the Karankawa Indians, a tribe of cannibals, who settled in the area. The menacing tribe, heavy with tattoos and piercings, would eat human flesh in the most astonishing way. The natives would tie prisoners of war to a stake, cut pieces of flesh from the victim's body, and cook it on a flame for consumption in front of their horrified captives.

The Spanish explorer Cabeza de Vaca called Galveston Island "Malhado", Spanish for "island of doom", because the Karankawa held him captive for much of his time in the area, but Cabeza de Vaca played a role in the island's "doomed" sprit. The discoverer came ashore in the 16th Century and floundered his way through the Americas, looking for new lands for the Spanish Empire. The explorer provided a map for future conquerors and the continued infiltration of the Spaniard armies, who killed and colonized their way across South and Central America, spilling indigenous blood in the name of Christ.

The veil of horror continued to cover Galveston into the 19th Century. Galveston provided harbor for slave trade and slave owners. In the presidential election of 1860, Abraham Lincoln did not receive a single vote in the town. The townspeople were violently opposed to Lincoln and his discussions of abolition. Political groups formed in Galveston to keep slave trade alive and keep out foreign immigrants. In addition, gangs formed to bully and pester immigrating fellow citizens, American citizens who had migrated from the northern United States to the south.

A hurricane hits Galveston directly every eight to nine years. I liken the barrage of devastating hurricanes that hit Galveston's coast as a Biblical bloodletting, like the flood, the great flood, constructed to wash away the sinful. The island has been completely underwater on several occasions because of hurricanes: 1857, 1867, twice in 1871, 1873, 1875 and 1877. And a hurricane that hit Galveston in 1900 is to date the deadliest natural catastrophe in the history of the United States, killing six thousand people. In comparison, the 1906 San Francisco Earthquake took seven hundred to three thousand lives, and the much-discussed Hurricane Katrina, which made landfall in New Orleans in 2005, was responsible for approximately 1,800 deaths. In 1910 a seawall was completed in Galveston in an attempt to save lives, but God continued to spill blood with deadly hurricanes in 1915, 1961, 1983 and 2008.

I have never thought of any devastating natural or terrorist event—anywhere—as an accident. A God does not create accidents. There is always a purpose. Normally during crushing times of crisis there is a wakeup call, which leads to beautiful displays of humanity and a restructuring of ideas and ideals. Well, Galveston has not changed; it still boils over with prejudice and lustful behavior. The town might appear to be a bustling little city with no hidden suspicions, catering to tourists and spring breakers, but a bleak history of violence still permeates into the township's present state of being. It is underfoot, everywhere one goes ... and here my husband and I go, descending into the eye of the storm.

JUNE 11, 2010

Lost. I am lost today. Because of yesterday.

Yesterday my husband and I arrived in Galveston around 7 p.m. The 285-mile drive from Dallas included a fight through Houston rush-hour traffic. The miles took their toll; they were stressful. Upon our arrival I needed a drink, fast.

We checked into our hotel, dropped our bags in our rooms, and went down to B. Jiggers Lounge, the hotel's attached club. I sailed into a series of drinks: a few beers followed by several margaritas, becoming inebriated quickly. My tension removed itself as I eased into a leisurely drunken state.

A six-piece cover band took the club's stage, and the atmosphere picked up as the musicians withered before me, tripping over a fast-paced

version of The Emotions' "Best of My Love".
Then—

An invading party of two arrived, finding the
only two empty seats in the club, the two seats
at our table. There were introductions, but my
head does not recall the specifics of the
conversation and their names still escape me; I
was too busy swimming in tequila and trying
my best to focus on a robotic version of
"Proud Mary".

From the beginning, the female in the
occupying party disgusted me. Pressed, greasy,
bent over into the face of my husband, smiling,
her teeth bleached an unnatural white, her face
a fabricated tanning salon orange. She traced
the intellectual contours of my husband as she
fenced him into a quiet conversation that I
could not hear over a continual line of
predictable songs. My husband smiled—
perpetually—and laughed—occasionally—as
she talked. While I watched them, the intruding
male in the party whispered in my ear. I could
feel the heat of his warm, wet breath. He talked
and I bobbed my head; I do not recall what he
was saying, but I was agreeing to something.

After several minutes of watching my husband
flirt—ignoring me—and nodding my head to a

dizzying collection of breezy words from the strange man—my brain cells wringed—I released myself into him. I left the table with the stranger, pushing past my husband, and continuing to push through to the dance floor. I remember holding the alien male's hands as we danced, strutting to "Superstition". The alien was nestled into me, grinding his midsection into mine, his tongue in my ear as I leaned over his shoulder, and then his tongue went in my mouth, sliding between my front teeth and lip. Essentially I was bartering my husband for this brief electrifying moment. I did not know my husband's location. I did not care.

The stranger and I decided to go to my hotel room, singing some absurd disco song along the way, kissing in the elevator, holding hands in the hall. When we arrived, my husband was already in the room, having a drink with the Martian female. He winked at me, flush with alcohol and something lustful. My strength and senses were waning, and then they went missing. Gone. I remember one fleeting moment when I ruminated on the concept of monogamy, something my husband and I had committed to on the day we married, and then it disappeared into a vortex of strange memories from long ago—something that sits, waiting, yet standing strong against me.

The room lights went off, and through the open curtains a few stray streams of luminosity dimly light our room. The female of the invading team took control immediately, seductively attacking my husband and driving him into a void, and the rest of the adventure was a four-part symphony.

The first movement was a vision of me sunken into the hotel mattress, the alien man heavy upon me; ecstasy enveloped on my face. The second part of the symphony—a tragic composition—was the cold empty room that my husband and I woke up to this morning, blood on the bed sheets from the alien's violent insurrection, our bags still unpacked on the floor, and the assailants vanished. The third section of the symphony was of me crying, kneeling in front of the commode and vomiting, refusing to be touched when my husband went to stroke my hair. The final division was the mark of rejection my husband felt, rejection that purloined his heart and split us in two.

JUNE 12, 2010

Dreary drips in Galveston.

We sit silently in our haunted hotel.
There is nothing to say.
There is nothing to imagine.

A stranger's presence is still very real.
The stupor. The starkness. The sting.
Boredom. Blood. Bile.

We have drowned.
In the water that surrounds our sorrows.
In Galveston.

JUNE 17, 2010

I left work yesterday at noon because I am currently unable to manage my emotions. For five days now I have been in a funk. I cannot eat. I cannot sleep. Minutes bite and bend and break. I am dehydrated and without energy; dark halos drain into my eyes, exploding into a staircase that takes me to spiderwebs on the basement floor. There is always a vision of Galveston in my head, taking me away from my basic instinct to survive. It is a vision of blood rushing over the seawall, which blocks Galveston from the riotous sea—riotous, a terror within me. I see myself floating in a thick, bubbling crimson bed of flowing ocean that overtakes the town's landscape. I am alive but barely. I see cannibal Indians. I see Spaniards breaking backs.

Yesterday, while sinking in the quick and struggling to free myself, I drove away from work. I do not remember the trip that took me thirty miles in the opposite direction of my home. I slept the entire way, waking abruptly when I veered into a parallel lane and almost sideswiped another car. The opposite car's horn provided my alarm.

I found myself in Fort Worth's cultural district. I parked. I saw cowgirls riding horses. I saw cowgirls smiling uneasy smiles. Fit upon their lips. Those terrible, scorched smiles told me dark secrets—those girls were ruined in some way. I've worn those smiles myself. I wear one right now.

Dig deeper.

I saw the vortex of Richard Serra's mind, and I climbed inside. I became a *waterfall inside a well*; my own private abyss as strands of my subdued internal laughter reverberated and collided into one another.

* * *

I am descending into a world where something supernatural controls my mind, and I am keenly aware that this force has no regard for my safety.

JUNE 18, 2010

Conversations. One needs them. In any good story.

For you.

Sitting on a bench in Dallas, One AT&T Plaza. My office is many stories of white stone and black glass above me. It is two hours after retiring for the day. Avoid my home; a void, my home. 9 p.m.

A man of privilege walks towards me like a rolling block.

He speaks. Yes, dialogue.

"Some change miss?"

He smells of human nature; it stands around him like its own entity. He is the smell of what we have learned to condemn, the scent of a person. The preference these days is for humans to smell like chemical flowers or laboratory fruit, the bark and oil of wood, tonka bean and sweet grass, vanilla and coco. We want to smell anything but human, the sinful smell of Homo sapiens.

"What for?" I ask.

"To live, woman. To live."

He squints his shark eyes as he says "to LIVE" the second time. The transparent jelly that smothers his dark iris and indistinguishable pupil bunches as he sells his life to me, as he narrows his eyes and moves past believing.

"And what are you living for?" I ask.

His arms, which are harnessed by a backpack and stretched to dirt-filled fingernails, drop and dangle in defeat. It is not supposed to be this hard, and his response tells me so.

"Yes or no? No is fine," he says with disdainful ease.

I stare through the hole in the man's jeans to the hole in his leg—an infection that eats everything, skin and hair—to the whole of his heart, a privileged heart. Hang on to nothing. If you are a void, you cannot fall into one. Avoid my home. A void is my home.

He walks away, leaving a trace of him behind, the outline of a weighty aura stained into the air. The unaesthetic odor of mortal moves away from me along with his clothes, which are wrinkled with waves of sweat and stapled onto his skeleton by humidity. His boat shoes, worn on one side from an irregular footfall, are a mark through the air as they move. The shoes belong to the twenty-six bones in each of his feet like horseshoes belong to horse hooves. But the important part of him is before me without density, an inkblot left behind in bright pink, a scented, luminous radiation that I collect. The collection of pink speaks to me: "I am among the last of the bohemians, a crack in the sidewalk."

The flesh of him hollers over his shoulder from several squares of sidewalk away: "Yes or no; it's simple."

I whisper into the broken collection of red on white before me: "I own you now, all of the beautiful independence that was gifted to me."

JUNE 20, 2010

I went to church this morning and waited for something to make sense:

Job 30

26 When I looked for good then evil came unto me: and when I waited for light, there came darkness. 27 My bowels boiled, and rested not: the days of affliction prevented me. 28 I went mourning without the sun: I stood up, and cried in the congregation. 29 I am a brother to dragons, and a companion to owls. 30 My skin is black upon me, and my bones are burned with heat. 31 My harp also turned to mourning, and my organ into the voice of them that weep.

JUNE 21, 2010

I awake to a chime.

A dim ray of light appears beckoning relentlessly.

The pit of me is gnarled and tangled.

The acid in my stomach is a reminder that I must go into another day shackled to a set of standards that everyone around me created without my consent.

JULY 4, 2010

Independence. It is true: independence is alive. My independence is a time warp that brings me to a systematic breakdown of time and space. I am in my car. I am driving. Again there is no memory of the distance between my departure and my arrival. Something always triggers an awakening: a police siren, a motorcycle skimming by me at 120 miles per hour, a near-collision, the end of a road. This time the coast of Texas is my alarm clock.

The humidity and the soggy smell of ocean tide remind me of Galveston, and a dense pain settles into the entirety of my upper torso, starting behind my sternum. However, this place is not Galveston; I know that much. Galveston is my enemy, and although one may not completely understand their enemy, one at least knows the intricate physical structure of their enemy. Definitely not Galveston, but it could be any other place along the ugly coastline of Texas.

I park in a gravel lot. Puddles of mud mark the territory. I get out of my car and walk in a zigzag between beaten beachcombers— hundreds of them—but they do not see me. The wind pushes heat. My skin is sticky. I think of my husband and I hear a toddler crying, hit sharply by a jellyfish sting. I think of my husband and I hear a baby crying, hit sharply by the melting clouds and the suffocating lock of what attempts to be air. I think of my husband and I hear a baby crying from the delicate folds of my intuition, from my womb, and all of a sudden, I need to know my location.

JULY 9, 2010

My location is a dilapidated corner of America, Corpus Christi. Infested with decay, everything in this coastal town appears antiquated and apathetic. Humidity's breath fogs sight, the sand blasts through all opposing objects, and the outline of the town is the grit and grime of oil refineries, drilling platforms, and barges. In this town, litter darts onto the beach by way of ocean, and litter darts into the ocean by way of beach. Buildings crumble in ways that do not immediately catch one's eyes, falling apart in bits. The city's buildings and homes are rounded and missing texture, mortar continuously resettles and spills bricks, white paint becomes a hostile yellow, and everything that is paved is a crack with dry vegetation poking through.

The days here bring out the physically decomposing shells of those who lack consciousness—the people of Corpus Christi—who droop within rotting flesh and open wounds, their eyes defiled and flat. They move with a slow, crawling step. The pretty people are ugly here. These disposables disappear when the night creeps over the land and water, hiding in their tombs as a task force of ghosts replaces them and occupies the whistling streets.

Corpus Christi is truly alive with only one thing: a contagious matter. As if struck by Yellow Fever (Yellow Jack, Black Vomit, American Plague), the inhabitants settle silently into despondence. The unremitting ailment makes simple tasks a chore, so the town dwellers leave the everyday jobs undone, and these undone responsibilities become a part of the unraveling body of Christ.

It is "it", the body of Christ, which reminds me that I must go home. My husband misses me and my doctor has news. Something is alive.

JULY 10, 2010

One month after my trip to Galveston, I am one month pregnant. When I look back to that dreadful night and the blood that wound its way from the tainted hearts of our one-off surrogate lovers, I now understand that the rich red paste came from the first incision of a life-altering surgery.

My hope set upon hope is that the brief sexual episode between my husband and I on that night in Galveston—when he took me from behind while I swam through red sheets and viscera—is the cause of my pregnancy. My husband and I did not immediately explore the other possibility, the possibility that my husband is not the father of the child.

It was not until later that night that my husband briefly mentioned to me that he might not have created the resident fetus. At the time when he tossed out the idea, my husband and I were settled into bed, looking through the television past some sitcom—dark shadows, long and mean, rose behind us from the radiating, VIBRATING box that watched us—while we dug deep into the nest of soft, white cotton that plumed around us. I did not respond to his comment. I did not even look at him, and he gently removed himself from the bed and disappeared daintily—daintily—into the dark hall. After a few minutes, I saw a low beam of light bend the black slightly, rearranging it into dark gray—but still as black as Tom Walker's devil. I waited a few minutes and then I went to find him.

He was in the kitchen with a glass of wine—wine—trembling, bracing himself as a deep dark cavity formed below his feet. My thoughts streamlined through my past, the seconds counting backwards to all the days before this day, to all the days that I have known this beautiful man—beautiful—who allowed me to be raped as he watched. I continued backwards in time, tracing the conduit before his existence in my life. Past the prescription drugs that controlled my state of being for many years because of an undefined bit of violence that protrudes from a dank villa in which Old Scratch sank low into the entrails all around me. Going backwards, gliding—slipping—all the way to the forming of my womb—my tainted womb—and back to my mother's womb, and to God, whose hands molded me into an unlikely libertine.

JULY 15, 2010

My medication has numbed me for so long that I can only remember a chain of very dull days. My imagination left me. And the purity of my senses went into hiding. So. I removed myself from my medicine five days ago. The numb? Is now a hum. A constant electrical surge. A rush that detonated my circuit box, leaving me exposed. Freedom.

And now the denizen of my womb is free from my toxic mixture of chemical remedy as well.

Wouldn't want to hurt the baby.

JULY 17, 2010

Clarity is not silent to me. It sounds off. It
hums. It is the sound your soul makes when
cleansed by baptism. Clarity is a sleep walk,
where the thinking is done for you, and you
follow an order. I have clarity. I have been
baptized by the realization that my existence
harbors a rotation of similar places and similar
people who are the enemy.

JULY 18, 2010

My aimless thoughts used to send me adrift and I would forget days. But now I remember "everything". Every millisecond of each day is stored in my head—not like a photograph—like moving film. And the soundtrack to this film is a buzz. An ever-present buzz. The same sort of buzz that a rabid animal must hear when it becomes hypersensitive to auditory and visual stimuli, after images and sounds collect at such a rapid pace, that the brain outgrows its cage.

JULY 19, 2010

I requested a leave of absence from my work.

I have to go. I have to depart my current surroundings for a time. To get my head straight. My house is haunted—my very first home in the beautiful Highland Park neighborhood of my youth is haunted—not by lost souls, but from the absence of a soul. My God is NOT there to protect my family and me, so I have to go find where the Holy Ghost has gone and bring It home.

JULY 26, 2010

I have been getting on planes and going nowhere. Flying into wherever. Transfers and boarding passes. Sleeping in airport terminals and bathing in airport sinks. Wandering into airport bars, sitting with the early-arrived and flight-delayed, avoiding eye contact with obnoxious business travelers who want to know my ins-and-outs, who have to talk, who have to embrace all of the people they encounter.

I have been through Denver Airport's New Belgium Hub Bar & Grill where I drank microbrews while immersing myself in bicycle paintings. Beleaguered, I settled into PDX's Laurelwood and pulled and pushed my way through its organic beer options. I fell asleep in Louisville's Woodford Reserve Bar & Grill after settling into one of their leather chairs and drinking several glasses of oak-aged bourbon. Finally, concourse B in Philadelphia gave me Cibo Bistro and Wine Bar, a stiff arena where I drank eight of their thirty-two wines and stumbled into a lopsided man at the long, onyx bar. I hung onto his silhouette as he dreamed me into a luxurious song, the first weary traveler with a soft voice. I squeezed that voice and I felt the place from where that voice came. SQUEEZED him gently on box springs. Squeezed him through the night. Waking up on the floor. Bits of him strangling my canvas. Red everywhere. Tones of him draped across the room's décor.

The Holy Spirit has been past these parts; it leaves its whisper behind, susurrating amidst the monotone of passing people, intercom directions and jet engines. I am several steps behind. I follow the haunting echo of its murmers out of the airport system and onto the trail of the open road.

I have not talked to my husband in a week.

JULY 27, 2010

Head full of spiders.

JULY 30, 2010

I drive and I see. It is stale and bitter all around me.

County Bank. Holiday Inn. Tanger Outlet. Tax-free liquor. Cracker Barrel. EconoLodge. KFC and A&W. Food Lion. Safeway. Comfort Inn.

A trembling hand delivers a handful of coins for a 9 a.m. Natural Light.

I keep finding my way to the coast. Shell shops and laundromats. Hermit crabs captured and called souvenirs.

Parking meters and parking passes needed to see the sand. Seagulls fishing for pretzels and potato chips. Airplanes destroying my view of the ocean with advertising banners.

A tapestry of tan lines and lines of tans.

We are dying.

JULY 31, 2010

Do they do it for the right reasons or for the spectacle? Eye-catching red and all golden. Tucked in stomachs and proper form, barely jiggling. They are steam rising from a hot pot, disappearing into the air. The many lionesses and the many lions.

AUGUST 1, 2010

I despise the ocean, I do. The sand, the smell, pretty people visiting ugly towns, molded into patterns of color. Umbrellas and towels. Chairs and plastic toys. The sun spoils in a painful gaze. It never really brings joy. Unrelenting, the grit. The shower of unclothed pretension. Societal murderers, rapists, and thieves all camouflaged as families.

AUGUST 2, 2010

Out of touch with everything but the ugly menace of peacocks nesting, roosting, tracing the contours of my lonely loins, tempting me.

AUGUST 3, 2010

Lincoln looks across the National Mall. He held the United States together like a magician and died for it, murdered, and now his long white, chalky image looks over dust kicking off shoes, a trample of people eating up a grotesque mix of grass and weeds and falling down fences.

He looks across a goat pasture on top of a gravel pit. Homeless people napping on paint-chipped benches as tourists from all over the world explore the contaminated cloud around them.

AUGUST 4, 2010

I am in the hills of West Virginia still searching for the Holy Ghost. I followed the trace of It here, and now It leaves me lonely.

There are buzzards swirling over a corpse way up in the Blue Mountains as the mist rises up to meet their ends. Somewhere in the middle there is lust, somewhere in the middle is me.

AUGUST 5, 2010

I caught myself hyperventilating today because of the lack of rhythm in my head. My mind used to play harp strings. A sort of gentle brushing of cords played me everyday. Now my head hears mass confusion. It is the sound of instruments being tuned all at once before a concert. Chaos.

AUGUST 6, 2010

I am at home.

Still absent of the Holy Ghost.

AUGUST 7, 2010

I am at work.

AUGUST 8, 2010

I am at Bally's health club in uptown Dallas. Avoiding home. A void is home. I am sitting in a reclining chair by the club's pool, which is outside on a roof that is three stories up. There are several swimming lanes in the pool and swimmers of differing levels of athletic ability occupy the straight shoots of water. The fifty meters of wet passage engage them and back-and-forth they wind into a tight muscle. There are sunbathers on the deck and all of them are male and presumably gay because homosexuals migrate to this part of Dallas called Oak Lawn. These lounging men are sodomites and they are all in denial of their future fate as sodium chloride fading in a fist of wind.

A young man does the backstroke. He transforms into the water itself as his chest rises and pounds. The pool rocks, throwing the less advanced swimmers in the other lanes off their parallel courses.

A dead animal bakes somewhere in the packaged landscaping that surrounds the pool. The smell is death soaking up the heat. I imagine maggots boring through the animal, frenzied, fighting for space inside a carcass, in the squared-off edges of a particularly thick, brilliant green bush.

We feed this bush a regular diet of refreshing, cold water from the tap, while someone in a refugee camp somewhere on this planet dies of dehydration. We manicure this bush like some high society slut, a makeover every week, and we perform this minor surgery on this plant so that it looks like a boxcar made out of a green sponge. A boxcar that nests a rotten animal and hides from the streets a row of sunbathing salt pillars in bikini trunks, sneering, bulging, ripped, tan and slick. Steadfast they appear with the visible eye, yet they blow in the wind.

Skyscrapers are set out around the rooftop pool like tombstones in a graveyard. Many office lights are still glowing, scattered here and there, in no particular pattern, sinking in the dull lake water of the polluted sky. People avoiding home; a void is their home. Falling occasionally, a star blinks to a close. The beaten worker heads home to insecurity, polygamy, porn, abuse and dysfunction, all held together by butterfly stitches. Inside the stitch is the smell of a corpse, a dead rodent of some sort with stained yellow teeth, hiding inside a hedge, which is soaking up nutrients and crisp, cold water. The stitch hides maggots that attach to death, sinking it into the earth behind a wall of green rectangle so thick it is impossible to capture or remove.

The powerful breaststroker pulls himself up onto the edge of the pool and takes a seat. He has a flawless chest, left arm, right arm, stomach, face, and hair. He is heaving with deep breaths and seems unbalanced as he reaches behind him to grab something, braces. He binds the braces to his dead legs, struggles to vault himself onto his incompatible, useless lower limbs, and limps past me with a horrible jerk.

A pillar of salt. A pillar of salt. A dissolving pillar of salt.

AUGUST 10, 2010

Two months ago I was raped while my husband watched.

SEPTEMBER 10, 2010

Three months ago I was raped by my husband.

OCTOBER 10, 2010

Four months ago I was raped by my husband and a stranger while an alien woman watched.

NOVEMBER 25, 2010

DECEMBER 25, 2010

JANUARY 1, 2011

FEBRUARY 10, 2011

Eight months ago I was murdered by a gang of three.

FEBRUARY 11, 2011

St. James.

The resurrected spirit of St. James fills me.

The original disciple of Jesus. A martyr.

FEBRUARY 14, 2011

I am a disguise.

* * *

This afternoon the unborn baby and I napped, snuggly wrapped within a hunter green comforter. My husband lay beside me for a minute. The view of us from the mirror was quite pleasant. His smile. His plump-cheeked face. His lashes for days. Brunette hair against a white pillow. How beautiful the baby will be.

He laid his head upon my raised tummy. I could feel his breath. I could hear his heart beat. Alive.

The fetus awoke and began to squirm inside her cocoon. Pushing against the fabric of my putrefaction.

I hope the child has my husband's big brown eyes. I hope she is clumsy like her stumbling father. I hope the child loves Scrabble and putting together puzzles like her father. I hope she hums when she is in the car with no radio on. I hope she loves to take naps. Watch the rain fall. Read three books at one time. Do *USA Today* crossword puzzles. Go to the horse races just to watch the horses run. All things that define her father.

Their glow is a fire that lights this room.

FEBRUARY 15, 2011

There was a sliver of promise when smiles were contagious and my imagination was not weight, but a means to navigate above hostile ground.

FEBRUARY 16, 2011

I am leaving for New York City today to work on the final edits of a training manual that I have been putting together for AT&T. Even at eight months pregnant, my work won't keep me in my home city. My boss will go to Hell for this.

FEBRUARY 17, 2011

I was in a meeting today. The lights were dim and there was a projection on a screen. Everyone was talking AT me. About halfway through the gathering, the room collapsed, and I imagined the space as a coffin with no escape. My pallbearers surrounded me in suits, coifs and veils.

Claustrophobia.

I took a deep breath and I thought of clean cuts of flesh. I thought of broad shoulders and a maze of freckles upon them. I closed my eyes and thought of an arched back and the nape of a severed neck.

It worked for a time.

Then I began to cut myself. Using a straightened paperclip, I made a starburst out of three lines while sitting in my high-dollar ergonomic leather chair.

The vice president of training called me to attention, and I unconsciously raised my arm to rest it on the table. Blood was running from the starburst. Everyone saw. No one said a word. The meeting was quickly adjourned. I grabbed my things and left.

FEBRUARY 18, 2011

There was a crowd of people stampeding towards home today, trying to beat an impending storm. They were in a zone, retreating in their thoughts as they jogged. I was in no hurry, walking loosely, undressing myself from my skin, impeding the pushing Manhattanites.

As I limply walked along, a rushing suit accidentally smacked my delicate pile of work from my hand. It fell to the ground, then was scattered by feet and wind. All I could see were black ink and red lines, corrections and changes, being trampled by shiny shoes, and swirling in the wind. The people around me immediately understood the dry piece of unfolding script—a dreary training manual—as "my work". And work in this city is life's blood.

In the drizzle, the people around me stopped. There was terror on their faces as they scurried for the missing parts, and then looks of charity about them as they handed each page back to me. They received no "thanks" from me because for a second, for the first time in so many days, there were not pages of angst pursuing me.

The crowd dispersed.

I put the collected papers in order as I walked to my hotel. I counted the pages as I did so.

Every page had made its way back to me. All 309 pages of the empty draft had found me once again.

FEBRUARY 19, 2011

A child is on the way.

FEBRUARY 20, 2011

I had imagined a different feeling. I had imagined a bond that escaped all doubt and established hope for what has become my rotting corpse. I had imagined that the bond between a mother and her offspring was instant and permanent. I had imagined that upon my first gaze at the baby as she was laid upon my chest that all divides would be bridged.

Instead there was no connection.

However, she is my progeny. And—

I cannot say if she is my husband's property. His glazed eyes certainly questioned the relationship. But a rouse did form as my husband tried to smile, acting his way into a kinship with the towhead, who looked upon his strange features and dark hair with wide eyes.

JAMES

MARCH 20, 2011

I met a guy named James today. He is a man who is full of vulnerability and a lot of heartbreak, but his liabilities are concealed by eyeliner, tattoos, and a chain of cigarettes.

I quickly found out that his mind is a mousetrap, an instrument of great design in its simplicity, presenting me with a small piece of instant gratification that is hooked to a neck breaking spring, a small piece of contentment that will undoubtedly lure me into an eternal trapping. Somehow that space—that trap—is the place that I need right now.

MARCH 21, 2011

I have been a sidewalk lately. I have buckled to trampling feet, but something delicate and precious has maneuvered through and is helping me strengthen my life with positive thoughts and ideas. Leveling my foundation and setting me up for my next great success when I was preparing for my next great failure.

There are so many wonderful things about James, but it is his heart and passion that I love the most. His heart does not just display moments of sultry heat and then falter into cold chasms; his heart is steady, always glowing warm. And it is mine for now. Mine: the heart of the son of thunder, who calls down fire from Heaven.

MARCH 26, 2011

James and I spent the night at a state park campground to escape our similar frenzied worlds. I woke up tangled around him in his tent. We were clinging to one another, pasted together because of the humidity. He was deep in sleep when I pulled myself from him. I sat up and hovered above his body, watching him breathe. His breaths were large, heavy, and violent as he passed through an intense dream.

Then I pulled the blanket back slowly and gazed at his naked, outstretched body. He's perfect, the most beautiful thing I have ever seen. Currently trimmed down to the basics, removed from his black clothes and eyeliner, he is delicate, soft, and translucent.

And he is mine, and there is pride in the thought that he is a trinket forward unto me. However, "mine" claims ownership, and while I am uncomfortable seeing him as a possession, I most certainly do, and I cannot escape the notion. I first felt that way yesterday while hiking. I grabbed James's hand to keep from falling down a short but steep slope, and then I lost my balance and fell into him. Goosebumps immediately formed across his skin and his nipples got hard. At that moment I had the unhealthy recognition, "I own you."

We rushed to the tent.

His lips. His body. His hair. Soaked and pulled behind his ears. His eyes. Glossy and frenetic. After a rapid rise and fall, we fell asleep with exhaustion.

It was a beautiful sleep.

I am learning so much about myself from him. I am learning about my capacity for lust and objectification, and it is painful to think of myself as such a shallow person.

MARCH 28, 2011

To have someone else performing for me after getting used to one seven-year act is as exhilarating as it is scary.

I have been in love with one man for the last seven years, but the past weekend's rendezvous starts a new beginning. My escape.

MARCH 29, 2011

I sat at home today and read, waiting for my move back to James, gritting my teeth, grinding. I do not remember a single word from the book that sat across my lap and unfolded in front of my eyes. The chapters did disappear, but the anticipation of seeing James tomorrow blocked any clear thinking. I could not absorb anything but him. What is that song? "Killing Me Softly"? I understand what those words mean now. There is another song by the Flaming Lips in which the lyrics recall: "the softest bullet ever shot." I have been shot, several times, but when?

I banged my head on the doorjamb today. Intentionally. I bled profusely as the jamb caught the soft part of the upper corner of my eye socket. As soon as the blood dripped across my lashes, I had a story already formulated about how it had occurred. It is a lame story in which I am the hero. Just something to share with James that doesn't involve the boring drudgery that is my life.

APRIL 1, 2011

It is amazing to see the child grow. Most mothers would be proud of those glimmering, shimmering eyes that look so much like the green sea of Galveston. She looks at me with adoration; she is hoodwinked.

While my husband is in the shower, I tell the baby about James. I tell her that I am lying to her father. I ask her if she still loves me. She smiles yes. I want James to meet the baby. But how? I have yet to explain that I have a baby. I have not gotten that far. My gut hurts to think about it.

In a few short hours, I will be in James's arms. He is staying with me at a hotel. I will not be coming home tonight. I will have my story straightened out by the time that my husband calls to question my whereabouts.

APRIL 2, 2011

I could not drive. That was the story that I told my husband. I drank too much while out with my girlfriends and I just could not drive. He offered to pick me up. I told him that I would sleep it off at a friend's house. He persisted. Over the course of a fifteen-minute battle of wills, I decided that I hated him. He was worried about my safety. I was worried about getting fucked. He accused me of being up to no good. I acted offended. I told him to go away. I hung up. I turned off my mobile phone. I returned to my hotel room. I fucked James for an hour. Then I sucked him clean. We took a thirty-minute break before we fucked again, fucking ourselves to sleep.

APRIL 3, 2011

James left the hotel to go home at 10 a.m., and then I was alone in the hotel room.

I looked for something sharp. I needed something sharp. I could not find anything sharp—floating around in the fucked up space in which I resided, not a happy hotel room anymore, just a lonely place with no personality or design, revolving around a numbing, bright light that took away the detail in everything, and I needed design and detail, and I needed something dark to take away the edge of the blinding white—so I broke the bathroom mirror with my fist. The impact of my fist against the solid glass surface did not hurt at that moment. I was floating in morphine as my endorphins collected, and I was not touching the ground when I took a piece of broken glass and cut the flap of flesh that hung over the misshapen knuckle of my right middle finger.

The busted-up hand—casted after a trip to the emergency room—saved me when I got home. The nurturer in my husband took over and he received me without a question. He did not want to know.

The emergency care seduced us both into a lustful state, something we had not experienced since Galveston, and we adjusted our mechanical routine to a brief bit of romance as he reclaimed me and my dirty pussy.

APRIL 4, 2011

I think that I am crying because I miss James. Confusion is settling into my chest. The pressure of my heart banging against my sternum is heavy.

I cannot eat.

When I stepped on the scale this morning, I realized that I had lost ten pounds since meeting James.

Missing sleep.

My internal scars are bursting through my skin in a bloody muddle.

My suffering is acceptable.

APRIL 5, 2011

Suffocation. Slapping. Objects inserted by force. Hair pulling—clumps of bloody hair in my fist.

Scar tissue is collecting where I bite the inside of my lip to release blood as I await James.

APRIL 7, 2011

It started with a phone call. James needed me. I met him in a gritty Mexican restaurant in the shitty shadows of the Dallas skyline. We drank several Margaritas and then he pulled me into the bathroom. He locked the door and sat me on the sink. He lifted my skirt. I was not wearing panties. He inserted his fingers. I was already wet. I was ready. He bit my neck hard and I liked that quite a bit. He lifted me off the sink, turned me around, and while fucking me from behind, he pushed my head against the sink. I asked him to stop pressing my head so hard, and he applied more force and then lifted my head and banged it violently against the porcelain basin as he came inside me. He then released me.

I gathered myself and sat on the toilet seat. My forehead was bruised and bleeding. He reached down to me and touched the blood. He looked sad. I smiled and grabbed a handful of toilet paper, wiping off the ichor from my head. We left out the back door without paying our tab.

"Will you hurt me now?" he asked on the way to the car.

"Later," I told him. "In time."

APRIL 20, 2011

I sat through the child's "two-months-old" birthday party with much distance. Where was I? I remember smiling for a moment as the baby sat in a mountain of crumpled gift-wrap. That is the only thing that I remember.

I rocked the baby to sleep after the party. Chubby cheeks. Full lips. Soft skin. An extreme, strange brand of love. A good baby, bubbly, always smiling, rarely crying, and when she does cry it is gentle and barely audible—strolling, rolling tears bigger than the sound.

Innocence.

I sobbed while examining her beauty. I thought of our distance in morality. Does she have bad thoughts? I have them all the time. I laid her in her crib and then fell asleep on the floor beside it. I needed to be in the presence of the guilt-free, of pure, sweet, mesmerizing innocence. I was hoping that her purity might fall down upon me, envelope me and make me better. Because I was sick. Sick and dying.

APRIL 21, 2011

My husband woke me in the morning with the baby in his arms. I told him that I did not love him anymore, which was the truth. I told him that we should go to counseling. He immediately made an appointment for tonight.

APRIL 22, 2011

The counseling session was a brush fire of lies.

* * *

I rarely think in concrete anymore. Most of my thoughts are a line between the surreal and abstract, and out on that ledge, I have truly begun to believe in a higher being. I yelled an abstract prayer to my abstract God today. It listened and shouted back abstract plans for me. It told me to save my life. It told me to free my demons, which are constructed of a surrender to blood and orgasmic secretions.

APRIL 23, 2011

James showed up unexpectedly at the doorstep of my home at about 10 p.m. last night. I invited him into my house. I left him loose clues as to my residence, as to my situation. He picked up on the hints.

I told him to have a seat on the couch in the living room. He was in a daze. It was unsettling. He sat down on the remote and the television clicked on to a commercial selling tampons. This sticks with me. That commercial about a menstruation product is still in my head. I remember it with clarity.

I sent my husband into the living room. I told the two men to talk. I went to the nursery and locked the door. I heard my husband crying. Then my husband was banging on the nursery door and screaming. I heard the front door open and slam. The crying stopped. I opened the door and walked past my husband's huddled mass. He grabbed my leg. I kicked his hand away. I walked to the backyard and took off my clothes. I jumped in the pool. It was startlingly cold. I breathed in water.

I awoke to a paramedic with his mouth on mine. My husband was holding my hand.

"You're so blue," he said.

I slept with my husband curled up into me. I slept. I slept for ten hours. I dreamed of a waterfall of blood and me a parasite, living off the waterfall's stream.

APRIL 24, 2011

I met James at a restaurant in Dallas.

He was picking at some lettuce and needing answers. I had none. But I wanted him. And he wanted me. He touched the scab on my forehead. It triggered anguish in me. It brought out the lust in him. Then my phone rang. My husband. He needed to work late, and he wanted me to pick up the baby from daycare. I snapped.

The next hour was a fog of mind travel across a blade.

Then I was at the daycare. Holding the baby tightly. Holding the baby too tightly. Squeezing. The nursery workers gave me a puzzled look as the baby squirmed. I released the pressure.

As I walked to my car, I cried onto the baby's small contingent of thin hair. She reached up and touched my tears. She looked amused. I noticed the spots of blood on the baby's hand first, then her face, and then I noticed spots of blood on my shirt. The spots were moving. Amoebas. Roaming chaotically. Before settling into a floating, stagnant constellation.

With the baby in my arms, and me in a stupor, I frantically dug through my purse to find my car keys—

But I found the sword of King Herod instead.

ESCAPE

APRIL 25, 2011

I did not sleep at all last night and I did not go to work today. I told my boss that I was dying, but in reality something is springing to life after years of oppression. But the accompanying insecurity of it all feels like death. There is heartbreak. There is fever. There is lust. There are chemicals. There are manifesting desires.

* * *

Three lines on my thigh. One in which I—accidentally—cut a little too deep. I was attempting to connect with physical hurt to ease my mental anguish, but the pain was dull all the way through.

Was I taking my body back? Was I reclaiming my cells after two years of a prescription drug-induced lobotomy?

The amount of blood lost was, well, simply amazing—a puddle formed on the plastic mat underneath my desk chair, a running slant in all directions.

APRIL 26, 2011

I was distant as I packed a few things. I was going to disappear for a while. My husband pleaded with me not to leave. I hit him with a sudden and abrupt backhand when he brought up James. A disappearing act.

My abstract God is pleading with me to stay as well. My abstract mind ignores the abstract notion of both It and my husband.

APRIL 27, 2011

I found myself wandering and wondering in the gritty part of downtown Dallas. There are three rows of streets—and everything in between—that mark a part of the city where the artsy, "alternative" crowd gathers; the locals call it Deep Ellum. It is the place one might find in any city where the "free" thinkers congregate, a "specific" area in which the "independent" people of the world hang out and "codepend" on one another.

Tattoo parlors, head shops, vintage stores, small music venues, bars.

I stepped into a place called July Alley—the black paint pealed in sections across my eyes to reveal vermillion—and sat down at the bar. I drank several Lone Star beers and a few vodka tonics in about an hour. I fell backwards off of my barstool, and the bartender quickly came to my rescue, helping me to my feet.

James. Smothered in amoebas. My martyr.

I rose, falling. The jukebox yelled at me to dance. The lights spoke to me in cadence, and I spun around in a haze as piss ran down my leg and into my shoes.

I found the door away from Bad Brains slamming its fist into me and hit the sidewalk. I smelled smoke as I obliquely pushed myself along through a mist. I came to the source of the smoke: a young man in black who blocked the way to my escape with a beguiling smile. He held a cigarette. We made eye contact.

"Hey," he said.

"Hey."

"Talk to me."

I followed his order and sat next to him on the sidewalk, against a throbbing concrete wall.

He offered his cigarette. I took it.

"Oh, you're all wet," he said.

I nodded my head and said, "I guess."

I took a drag of mostly filter. Blew smoke.

"I saw you in July Alley," he said.

"Quite a scene."

"Lame, really. Scene-stealing, scene queen, scenesters."

"With a strict dress code."

"Very strict. Image focused. Vain. A uniform piece of mainstream society. The only desire of the scenester is to create a stage so that hipsters have something to do. The hipsters, of course, being the scenester's bitch."

"Thanks for destroying humanity for me."

I sighed, got up.

"Where are you going?" he asked.

"I haven't really thought about it."

I stared at him. Dropped the cigarette. Crushed it.

"I want to come with you," he said.

"Come. Take me somewhere."

We left. We hopped into his car. We were on Greenville Avenue. We were filled with alcohol. Libertine. And beyond. A strange bar where we exchanged rhymes with the locals for ice diamonds and alcohol.

We were in the street. We were kissing. Rain started to fall. I could not get enough of his tongue. His hair was in my hands. I was bound by him—his slender arms and his ferocious nails.

Dark.

He pulled away. He breathed heavily. Rain fell across his face. His eyes were feral. Green. Luminous.

A panther.

"You drain me," he said. "Do you know what you do to people?"

He grabbed my hand and pulled me down the sidewalk. We moved between two buildings and he was all the way into me. I was pink. There was magic everywhere as it continued to rain soft bullets.

I was alone.

I ended up in a place that I had not been to in years. The same people were still there, lurking and staring at a lone pool table. Their fists held tight a revolving glass; their mouths drooped into submission. Their skin color had faded to gray; their makeup not so much. They told me that I looked great, but the way in which they said it was a terrible lie.

Everyone got thinner until they eventually faded into the room's paneling.

I was alone.

I was in a parking lot and then a field. I fell in the wet grass and stayed there on my back, shivering. I looked up into a dark cloudless sky and saw a stagnant sea. I wondered where the stars had gone. They once dominated my every night until a line was crossed and innocence was lost.

Disappearer.

Stars fade in the bright lies of the world.

The glow is greater than the illumination of our hearts.

A pale recollection.

APRIL 28, 2011

I do not fall asleep but I wake up. It is midnight. I find a bar. I am so hungry. I am shaking.

A man with rosy nostrils holds my hand from his post next to me. He is trembling. Twisting.

I do not sleep but I wake up. It is 3 a.m. A man tells me that I am a never-ending heartache and then he lands successfully.

I do not sleep but I wake up. It is noon.

I am alone.

I think of the man. Defenseless. Bloodshot. Lustful.

I do not sleep but I wake up. It is midnight. I find a bar. I hunger. I shake. A man sings me a song. He is quivering. Twitching. Flickering. There is just enough light to see.

MAY 2, 2011

Between you and me, there is about two feet of floor. From the bed where I sprawl to the desk where you work. And in only three days you find the distance too much, so you claw at me, and then I slide into your lap. Your lankiness against me is as oppressive as the rigid kisses you tender as gifts.

You were looking for a guy, but instead you found a girl who is just as sweet, just as tasty, and so we are here, living in this proximity for three days now. The vodka went first, then the whiskey, then the tequila, and now we are reduced to gin and hot beer.

I use the numbness within me to create space. You use it for attention. You ask about my scars, but I refuse to go that deep with you. So our conversations are of the mundane, talks of Iggy Pop and Austin. And we watch television and dissolve.

I wake up with a headache, going on day four, and I am not sure, exactly, where you have gone.

The smell of the room is horrific. There are new designs to ponder for the territory has been marked by a wraith.

MAY 3, 2011

I pick up a brochure to find that I am in an extended stay hotel in Houston. There is a stream of vomit trailing from the bed to a curled up ball of human in the open space underneath the sink. I recall a name. Jasmine? She is naked, her eyes are swollen shut, her nose is a knot and straining to breathe. It appears that her arms and legs are casualties to compound fractures.

I think of the baby. I miss her.

MAY 31, 2011

I show up at my house at midnight. There is an unfamiliar car in the driveway. I key the gray BMW as I walk by it. My key still works the lock on the house door. I open it. I head to the master bedroom. The form of two bodies lies under a pastel blue sheet. I attack the smaller form. In just a few seconds, a woman is so bloody that red consumes her face. I look down at her bursting eyes as my husband pulls my arm. The woman's mouth is stretched to a scream, but she is mute to me. I look to the fan above us because it calls my name. I hear it. I hear the fan, but not her.

I go to the nursery to see the baby while my husband attends to his whore. I pick up the child, and she buries her head into my shoulder. I give her a quick hug and then set her back in her crib. She reaches for me. She starts to cry. I tell her that I love her more than anything in the world. I tell her to be good. I kiss her crown. I grab a framed picture of her and leave the house. I drive down a highway until I run out of gas. I walk into the woods and continue to hike until the sun comes up.

I fall asleep.

JUNE 1, 2011

I wake up shivering, resting on a bed of soggy leaves. Chigger bites and scratches cover me. I am clutching the baby's framed picture against my chest. I get up and walk until I find myself on a farm-to-market road. I thumb down a car and it takes me to a bus stop. The next bus out is headed to Arizona. I buy a ticket.

JUNE 2, 2011

It is 4 a.m. and the bus shivers along. The people around me are rotting. Shifting uncomfortably in their seats and melting into their cushions. Except for my neighbor, who is sleeping peacefully. A bouquet of mangled and droopy flowers is at her feet. She falls a bit towards me as she slumbers, and I can hear the drone of techno music in her headphones. I put my arm around her and I rest my head against hers, falling asleep too.

I awake to a strike of light, which plunges across a desert haze and through the front bus window. My neighbor is gone. She has moved two rows up to an empty seat.

I stay on the bus, paying to go past Arizona to the young woman's destination because wherever she lives, I live now.

The bus stops about seven hours later and she gathers her things. She looks behind to me and then begins to leave the bus. I follow her. I am not sure what city I am in right now.

I catch up to her. I ask her for her name and it is a paradox. Lacy she is not. She is metal spikes and leather. I see it.

She is a liar.

After I stare at her with nothing to say for several seconds, she rolls her eyes and walks away from me. I continue to follow her. She turns to me.

"Are you crazy?" she asks. "Will you leave me alone?"

"What's crazy about me?"

She looks me up and down. Scratches from thorn bushes zigzag across me. My bug bites keep me itching and blood runs from dozens of small scabs. My shirt has a splash of dry blood upon it. She cocks her head. I giggle.

"I get it," I say.

She walks away again, and this time I stand at a distance and watch a group of people take turns hugging her—family, friends.

My taxi is right on her tail. The taxi continues forward as the car she occupies stops in a middle class neighborhood. I write down the address.

I go to a hotel. I turn on the television. Time to heal.

JUNE 9, 2011

I have not seen the light of day in a week. The shades are drawn, as I get better. Feeling better. As my physical appearance improves, I feel emotionally fit. Is this a mistake? I say this because I feel so heavy until—

I am watching *The Shining*, and as blood pours from the elevator doors in one of the scenes, I find myself cheering. I am two feet from the television and I am clapping and laughing.

TRANSFORMATION

JUNE 10, 2011

I had the best intentions.

An abnormally hot day rested upon me as I penned thoughts in my journal, my back resting against a tree. And then there was a man in my scopes. Running, playing tag with his dog, and then rolling with his retriever in the grass. Then they disappeared, or so I thought.

A wet nose found my ear. Then a lick across my face. Then the dog's owner was there in front of me in black shorts and a tank top.

"Sorry," the man said.

"No need."

"She seems to like you."

And I thought, "Why?"

Don't dogs have that innate mechanism within them that gives them the ability to pick out bad sorts? Maybe the dog didn't pick up my regular rhythm because as I mentioned, I had the best intentions.

JUNE 11, 2011

I am in California. I am standing on the beach. The ocean generates soup, a white foamy creation. The moon is low, and its tail on the water is in constant motion. It is a sperm grabbing an egg. I see a glowing satellite, and I follow it with my eyes until it goes behind a large hotel on the shore. There are people on the hotel's pool deck, and I hear music. Salsa.

I walk to the deck and peer at the drunken people—in motion, flying to the beat of a Fania All Stars's song, a frat party for forty-year-olds. I hop the fence and go to the bar. I order a vodka tonic. I drink it in one gulp. I order another. And then several more. It hits me all at once, right as a musical transition occurs. Still the Fania All Stars, but no longer salsa— instead, a lullaby. From *Rosemary's Baby*.

Everyone shuts down and moves to the side of the dance floor while *I have a dream of someone raping me. I think it was someone inhuman.*

I move to the middle of the dance floor and sashay about. I get dizzy and stumble sideways off of the dance floor. A man in a suit grabs me. He asks to see my room key. From my pocket I produce a handful of teeth. I offer them to him. He looks startled.

"I collect them," I say. "I am working on a necklace."

He walks me through the lobby and tells me to leave the premises. I nod my head in acknowledgment of his wishes. I cross the street into a residential neighborhood of wood-framed houses. I stagger, fall, and crawl between two homes. I look into the sky. The stars are moving. Many satellites. I fall asleep. An ashen nightmare.

I am awoken in the early morning by a police officer and a man in a robe. The cop asks me for identification. I show it to him.

"You're a long way from home," he says.

"I am on vacation."

He asks where I am staying. I produce a receipt for a hotel.

"You're a long way from your hotel," he says.

"Bad night," I say.

He drives me to my hotel and drops me off. I thank him. I pull out a key card from my wallet and find its room. I open the door. There is a dead dog on the floor. He is gutted and his innards make a trail for several feet.

Who put that there?

I go the bathroom and there is a petite man in the bathtub. He is gagged. He is tied. He is naked. He is missing his nose. His eyes are alive.

JUNE 12, 2011

XXXXXXXXXXXXXXXXXXXXXXXXXXXXX
XXXXXXXXXXXXXXXXXXXXXXXXXXXXX
XXXXXXXXXXXXXXXXXXXXXXX I wake up.
XXXXXXXXXXXXXXXXXXXXX In the same
clothes. XXXXXXXXXXXXXXXXXXXXXXXX
XX I put on yesterday. XXXXXXXXXX I itch.
XXXXXXXXXX I move without rhythm. XX
XXXXXXXXXXXXXXXXXXXXXXXXXXXXX
XXXXXXXXXXXXXXXXXXXXXXXXXXXXX
XXXXXXXXXXXXXXXXXXXXXXXXXXXXX
XXXXX I meet you. XXXXXXXXXX In the
street. XXXXXXXXXXXXXXXXXXXXXXXX
XXXXXXXXXXXXXXXXXXXXXXXXXXXXX
XXXXXXXXXXXXXXX We're both wrinkled.
XXXXX Weathered. XXXXXXXXXXXXXX
And all upside down. XXXXXXXXXXXXXX
XXXXXXXXXXXXXXXXXXXXXXXXXXXXX
XXXXXXXXXXXXXXX A transfer takes place.

XXXXXXXXXXXXXXXXXXXXXXXXXXXXXX
XXXXXXXXXXXXXXXXXXXXXXXXXXXXXX
XXXXXXXXXXXXXXXXXXX You want. XX
XXXXXX To be comfortable. XXX One day.
XXXXXXXXXXXXXXXXXXXXXXXXXXXXXX
XXXXXXXXXXXXXXXXXXXXXXXXXXXXXX
XXXXXXXXXXXXXXXXXXXXXXXXXXXXXX
XXXXXXXXXX You want. XXXXXXXXXX
XXXXXXXXXXXXXXXXXXXX A little slack.
XXXXXXXXXXXXXXXXXXXXXXXXXXXXXX
XXXXXXXXXXXXXXXXXXXXXXXXXXXXXX
XXXXXXXX Shimmer gets you taut. XXXXX
XXXXXXXXXXXXXXXXXXXXXXXXXXXXXX
XXX I introduce you. XXX To the thought. X
XXXXXXXXXXXXXXXXXXXXXXXXXXXXXX
XXXXXXXXXXXXXXXXXXXX Your smile.
Lifted to one side. XXXXXXXXXXXXXXXXX
You are so careless. XXXXXXXXXXXXXXX
With it. XXXX Your kind words. XXXXXXX
The way you look. XXXX At me. XXXXXXX
XXXXXXXXXXXXXXXXXXXXXX Deception.
XXXXXXXXXXXXXXXXXXXXXXXXXXXXXX
XXXXXXXXXXXXXXXXXXXXXXXXXXXXXX
XXXXXXXXXXXXXXXXXXXXXXXXXXXXXX
XXXXXXXXXXXXXXXXXXXXXXXXXXXXXX

XXXXXXXXXXXXXXXXXXXXXXXXXXX
XXXXXXXXXXXXXXXXXXXXXXXXXXX
XXXXXXXXXXXXXXXXXXXX An exorcism
takes place. XXXXXXXXXXXXXXXXXXXXX
A fighting. XXXXXXXXXXXXXXX Flailing.
XXXXXXXXXXXXXXXXXX Demon appears.
XXXXXXXXXXXXXXXXXXXXXXXXXXX
XXXXXXXXXXXXXXXXXXXXXXXXXXX
XXXXXXXXXXXXXXXXXXXXXXXXXXX
XXXXXXXXXXXXXXXXXXXXXXXXXXX
XXXXXXXXXXXXXXXXXXXXXXXXXXX
XXXXXXXXXX With all the hate. XXXXXXX
XXXXXXXXXXXXXXXXXX Of a hurricane.
The last thing you see: XXXXXXXXXXXXX
XXXXXXXXXXXXXXXXXXXXXXXXXXX
XXXXXXXXXXXXX Bursting, blazing veins.
XXXXXXXXXXXXXXXXXXXXXXXXXXX
XXXXXXXXXXXXXXXXXXXXXXXXXXX
XXXXXXXXXXXXXXXXXXXXXXXXXXX
XXXXXXXXXXXXXXXXXXXXXXXXXXX
XXXXXXXXXXXXXXXXXXXXXXXXXXX
XXXXXXXXXXXXXXXXXXXXXXXXXXX
XXXXXXXXXXXXXXXXXXXXXXXXXXX
XXXXXXXXXXXXXXXXXXXXXXXXXXX
XXXXXXXXXXXXXXXXXXXXXXXXXXX

XXXXXXXXXXXXXXXXXXXXXXXXX
XXXXXXXXXXXXXXXXXXXXXXXXX
XXXXXXXXXXXXXXXXXXXXXXXXX
XXXXXXXXXXXXXXXXXXXXXXXXX
XXXXXXXXXXXXXXXXXXXXXXXXX
XXXXXXXXXXXXXXXXXXXXXXXXX
XXXXXXXXXXXXXXXXXXXXXXXXX
XXXXXXXXXXXXXXXXXXXXXXXXX
XXXXXXXXXXXXXXXXXXXXXXXXX
XXXXXXXXXXXXXXXXXXXXXXXXX
XXXXXXXXXXXXXXXXXXXXXXXXX
XXXXXXXXXXXXXXXXXXXXXXXXX
XXXXXXXXXXXXXXXXXXXXXXXXX
XXXXXXXXXXXXXXXXXXXXXXXXX
XXXXXXXXXXXXXXXXXXXXXXXXX
XXXXXXXXXXXXXXXXXXXXXXXXX
XXXXXXXXXXXXXXXXXXXXXXXXX
XXXXXXXXXXXXXXXXXXXXXXXXX
XXXXXXXXXXXXXXXXXXXXXXXXX
XXXXXXXXXXXXXXXXXXXXXXXXX
XXXXXXXXXXXXXXXXXXXXXXXXX
XXXXXXXXXXXXXXXXXXXXXXXXX
XXXXXXXXXXXXXXXXXXXXXXXXX

XXXXXXXXXXXXXXXXXXXXXXXXXX
XXXXXXXXXXXXXXXXXXXXXXXXXX
XXXXXXXXXXXXXXXXXXXXXXXXXX
XXXXXXXXXXXXXXXXXXXXXXXXXX
XXXXXXXXXXXXXXXXXXXXXXXXXX
XXXXXXXXXXXXXXXXXXXXXXXXXX
XXXXXXXXXXXXXXXXXXXXXXXXXX
XXXXXXXXXXXXXXXXXXXXXXXXXX
XXXXXXXXXXXXXXXXXXXXXXXXXX
XXXXXXXXXXXXXXXXXXXXXXXXXX
XXXXXXXXXXXXXXXXXXXXXXXXXX
XXXXXXXXXXXXXXXXXXXXXXXXXX
XXXXXXXXXXXXXXXXXXXXXXXXXX
XXXXXXXXXXXXXXXXXXXXXXXXXX
XXXXXXXXXXXXXXXXXXXXXXXXXX
XXXXXXXXXXXXXXXXXXXXXXXXXX
XXXXXXXXXXXXXXXXXXXXXXXXXX
XXXXXXXXXXXXXXXXXXXXXXXXXX
XXXXXXXXXXXXXXXXXXXXXXXXXX
XXXXXXXXXXXXXXXXXXXXXXXXXX
XXXXXXXXXXXXXXXXXXXXXXXXXX
XXXXXXXXXXXXXXXXXXXXXXXXXX
XXXXXXXXXXXXXXXXXXXXXXXXXX
XXXXXXXXXXXXXXXXXXXXXXXXXX

XXXXXXXXXXXXXXXXXXXXXXXXXXXXXXXX
XXXXXXXXXXXXXXXXXXXXXXXXXXXXXXXX
XXXXXXXXXXXXXXXXXXXXXXXXXXXXXXXX
XXXXXXXXXXXXXXXXXXXXXXXXXXXXXXXX
XXXXXXXXXXXXXXXXXXXXXXXXXXXXXXXX
XXXXXXXXXXXXXXXXXXXXXXXXXXXXXXXX
XXXXXXXXXXXXXXXXXXXXXXXXXXXXXXXX
XXXXXXXXXXXXXXXXXXXXXXXXXXXXXXXX
XXXXXXXXXXXXXXXXXXXXXXXXXXXXXXXX
XXXXXXXXXXXXXXXXXXXXXXXXXXXXXXXX
XXXXXXXXXXXXXXXXXXXXXXXXXXXXXXXX
XXXXXXXXXXXXXXXXXXXXXXXXXXXXXXXX
XXXXXXXXXXXXXXXXXXXXXXXXXXXXXXXX
XXXXXXXXXXXXXXXXXXXXXXXXXXXXXXXX
XXXXXXXXXXXXXXXXXXXXXXXXXXXXXXXX
XXXXXXXXXXXXXXXXXXXXXXXXXXXXXXXX
XXXXXXXXXXXXXXXXXXXXXXXXXXXXXXXX
XXXXXXXXXXXXXXXXXXXXXXXXXXX Mine own
XXXXXXXXXXXXXXXXXXXXXXXX familiar friend
XXXXXXXXXXXXXXXXXXXXXX in whom I trusted
XXXXXXXXXXXXXXXXXXXXXXXX which did eat
XXXXXXXXXXXXXXXXXXXXXXXXX of my bread
XXXXXXXXXXXXXXXXXXXXXXXXX hath lifted up
XXXXXXXXXXXXXXXXXXXXX his heel against me.
XXXXXXXXXXXXXXXXXXXXXXXXXXXXXXXX
XXXXXXXXXXXXXXXXXXXXXXXXXXXXXXXX
XXXXXXXXXXXXXXXXXXXXXXXXXXXXXXXX
XXXXXXXXXXXXXXXXXXXXXXXXXXXXXXXX
XXXXXXXXXXXXXXXXXXXXXXXXXXXXXXXX
XXXXXXXXXXXXXXXXXXXXXXXXXXXXXXXX
XXXXXXXXXXXXXXXXXXXXXXXXXXXXXXXX
XXXXXXXXXXXXXXXXXXXXXXXXXXXXXXXX
XXXXXXXXXXXXXXXXXXXXXXXXXXXXXXXX
XXXXXXXXXXXXXXXXXXXXXXXXXXXXXXXX

XXXXXXXXXXXXXXXXXXXXXXXXXXXXXXXXXXXXXX
XXXXXXXXXXXXXXXXXXXXXXXXXXXXXXXXXXXXXX
XXXXXXXXXXXXXXXXXXXXXXXXXXXXXXXXXXXXXX
XXXXXXXXXXXXXXXXXXXXXXXXXXXXXXXXXXXXXX
XXXXXXXXXXXXXXXXXXXXXXXXXXXXXXXXXXXXXX
XXXXXXXXXXXXXXXXXXXXXXXXXXXXXXXXXXXXXX
XXXXXXXXXXXXXXXXXXXXXXXXXXXXXXXXXXXXXX
XXXXXXXXXXXXXXXXXXXXXXXXXXXXXXXXXXXXXX
XXXXXXXXXXXXXXXXXXXXXXXXXXXXXXXXXXXXXX
XXXXXXXXXXXXXXXXXXXXXXXXXXXXXXXXXXXXXX
XXXXXXXXXXXXXXXXXXXXXXXXXXXXXXXXXXXXXX
XXXXXXXXXXXXXXXXXXXXXXXXXXXXXXXXXXXXXX
XXXXXXXXXXXXXXXXXXXXXXXXXXXXXXXXXXXXXX
XXXXXXXXXXXXXXXXXXXXXXXXXXX Satan entered into him.
XXXXXXXXXXXXXXXXXXXXXXXXXXXXXXXXXXXXXX
XXXXXXXXXXXXXXXXXXXXXXXXXXXXXXXXXXXXXX
XXXXXXXXXXXXXXXXXXXXXXXXXXXXXXXXXXXXXX
XXXXXXXXXXXXXXXXXXXXXXXXXXXXXXXXXXXXXX
XXXXXXXXXXXXXXXXXXXXXXXXXXXXXXXXXXXXXX
XXXXXXXXXXXXXXXXXXXXXXXXXXXXXXXXXXXXXX
XXXXXXXXXXXXXXXXXXXXXXXXXXXXXXXXXXXXXX
XXXXXXXXXXXXXXXXXXXXXXXXXXXXXXXXXXXXXX
XXXXXXXXXXXXXXXXXXXXXXXXXXXXXXXXXXXXXX
XXXXXXXXXXXXXXXXXXXXXXXXXXXXXXXXXXXXXX
XXXXXXXXXXXXXXXXXXXXXXXXXXXXXXXXXXXXXX
XXXXXXXXXXXXXXXXXXXXXXXXXXXXXXXXXXXXXX
XXXXXXXXXXXXXXXXXXXXXXXXXXXXXXXXXXXXXX
XXXXXXXXXXXXXXXXXXXXXXXXXXXXXXXXXXXXXX
XXXXXXXXXXXXXXXXXXXXXXXXXXXXXXXXXXXXXX
XXXXXXXXXXXXXXXXXXXXXXXXXXXXXXXXXXXXXX
XXXXXXXXXXXXXXXXXXXXXXXXXXXXXXXXXXXXXX
XXXXXXXXXXXXXXXXXXXXXXXXXXXXXXXXXXXXXX
XXXXXXXXXXXXXXXXXXXXXXXXXXXXXXXXXXXXXX
XXXXXXXXXXXXXXXXXXXXXXXXXXXXXXXXXXXXXX
XXXXXXXXXXXXXXXXXXXXXXXXXXXXXXXXXXXXXX
XXXXXXXXXXXXXXXXXXXXXXXXXXXXXXXXXXXXXX
XXXXXXXXXXXXXXXXXXXXXXXXXXXXXXXXXXXXXX

XXXXXXXXXXXXXXXXXXXXXXXXXXXXXXXXXXXXXXXXXX
XXXXXXXXXXXXXXXXXXXXXXXXXXXXXXXXXXXXXXXXXX
XXXXXXXXXXXXXXXXXXXXXXXXXXXXXXXXXXXXXXXXXX
XXXXXXXXXXXXXXXXXXXXXXXXXXXXXXXXXXXXXXXXXX
XXXXXXXXXXXXXXXXXXXXXXXXXXXXXXXXXXXXXXXXXX
XXXXXXXXXXXXXXXXXXXXXXXXXXXXXXXXXXXXXXXXXX
XXXXXXXXXXXXXXXXXXXXXXXXXXXXXXXXXXXXXXXXXX
XXXXXXXXXXXXXXXXXXXXXXXXXXXXXXXXXXXXXXXXXX
XXXXXXXXXXXXXXXXXXXXXXXXXXXXXXXXXXXXXXXXXX
XXXXXXXXXXXXXXXXXXXXXXXXXXXXXXXXXXXXXXXXXX
XXXXXXXXXXXXXXXXXXXXXXXXXXXXXXXXXXXXXXXXXX
XXXXXXXXXXXXXXXXXXXXXXXXXXXXXXXXXXXXXXXXXX
XXXXXXXXXXXXXXXXXXXXXXXXXXXXXXXXXXXXXXXXXX
XXXXXXXXXXXXXXXXXXXXXXXXXXXXXXXXXXXXXXXXXX
XXXXXXXXXXXXXXXXXXXXXXXXXXXXXXXXXXXXXXXXXX
XXXXXXXXXXXXXXXXXXXXXXXXXXXXXXXXXXXXXXXXXX
XXXXXXXXXXXXXXXXXXXXXXXXXXXXXXXXXXXXXXXXXX
XXXXXXXXXXXXXXXXXXXXXXXXXXXXXXXXXXXXXXXXXX
XXXXXXXXXXXXXXXXXXXXXXXXXXXXXXXXXXXXXXXXXX
XXXXXXXXXXXXXXXXXXXXXXXXXXXXXXXXXXXXXXXXXX
XXXXXXXXXXXXXXXXXXXXXXXXXXXXXXXXXXXXXXXXXX
XXXXXXXXXXXXXXXXXXXXXXXXXXXXXXXXXXXXXXXXXX
XXXXXXXXXXXXXXXXXXXXXXXXXXXXXXXXXXXXXXXXXX
XXXXXXXXXXXXXXXXXXXXXXXXXXXXXXXXXXXXXXXXXX
XXXXXXXXXXXXXXXXXXXXXXXXXXXXXXXXXXXXXXXXXX
XXXXXXXXXXXXXXXXXXXXXXXXXXXXXXXXXXXXXXXXXX
XXXXXXXXXXXXXXXXXXXXXXXXXXXXXXXXXXXXXXXXXX
XXXXXXXXXXXXXXXXXXXXXXXXXXXXXXXXXXXXXXXXXX
XXXXXXXXXXXXXXXXXXXXXXXXXXXXXXXXXXXXXXXXXX
XXXXXXXXXXXXXXXXXXXXXXXXXXXXXXXXXXXXXXXXXX
XXXXXXXXXXXXXXXXXXXXXXXXXXXXXXXXXXXXXXXXXX
XXXXXXXXXXXXXXXXXXXXXXXXXXXXXXXXXXXXXXXXXX
XXXXXXXXXXXXXXXXXXXXXXXXXXXXXXXXXXXXXXXXXX
XXXXXXXXXXXXXXXXXXXXXXXXXXXXXXXXXXXXXXXXXX
XXXXXXXXXXXXXXXXXXXXXXXXXXXXXXXXXXXXXXXXXX
XXXXXXXXXXXXXXXXXXXXXXXXXXXXXXXXXXXXXXXXXX
XXXXXXXXXXXXXXXXXXXXXXXXXXXXXXXXXXXXXXXXXX
XXXXXXXXXXXXXXXXXXXXXXXXXXXXXXXXXXXXXXXXXX

XXXXXXXXXXXXXXXXXXXXXXXXXXXXXXXXXXXXXXXXXXXXXXXX
XXXXXXXXXXXXXXXXXXXXXXXXXXXXXXXXXXXXXXXXXXXXXXXX
XXXXXXXXXXXXXXXXXXXXXXXXXXXXXXXXXXXXXXXXXXXXXXXX
XXXXXXXXXXXXXXXXXXXXXXXXXXXXXXXXXXXXXXXXXXXXXXXX
XXXXXXXXXXXXXXXXXXXXXXXXXXXXXXXXXXXXXXXXXXXXXXXX
XXXXXXXXXXXXXXXXXXXXXXXXXXXXXXXXXXXXXXXXXXXXXXXX
XXXXXXXXXXXXXXXXXXXXXXXXXXXXXXXXXXXXXXXXXXXXXXXX
XXXXXXXXXXXXXXXXXXXXXXXXXXXXXXXXXXXXXXXXXXXXXXXX
XXXXXXXXXXXXXXXXXXXXXXXXXXXXXXXXXXXXXXXXXXXXXXXX
XXXXXXXXXXXXXXXXXXXXXXXXXXXXXXXXXXXXXXXXXXXXXXXX
XXXXXXXXXXXXXXXXXXXXXXXXXXXXXXXXXXXXXXXXXXXXXXXX
XXXXXXXXXXXXXXXXXXXXXXXXXXXXXXXXXXXXXXXXXXXXXXXX
XXXXXXXXXXXXXXXXXXXXXXXXXXXXXXXXXXXXXXXXXXXXXXXX
XXXXXXXXXXXXXXXXXXXXXXXXXXXXXXXXXXXXXXXXXXXXXXXX
XXXXXXXXXXXXXXXXXXXXXXXXXXXXXXXXXXXXXXXXXXXXXXXX
XXXXXXXXXXXXXXXXXXXXXXXXXXXXXXXXXXXXXXXXXXXXXXXX
XXXXXXXXXXXXXXXXXXXXXXXXXXXXXXXXXXXXXXXXXXXXXXXX
XXXXXXXXXXXXXXXXXXXXXXXXXXXXXXXXXXXXXXXXXXXXXXXX
XXXXXXXXXXXXXXXXXXXXXXXXXXXXXXXXXXXXXXXXXXXXXXXX
XXXXXXXXXXXXXXXXXXXXXXXXXXXXXXXXXXXXXXXXXXXXXXXX
XXXXXXXXXXXXXXXXXXXXXXXXXXXXXXXXXXXXXXXXXXXXXXXX
XXXXXXXXXXXXXXXXXXXXXXXXXXXXXXXXXXXXXXXXXXXXXXXX
XXXXXXXXXXXXXXXXXXXXXXXXXXXXXXXXXXXXXXXXXXXXXXXX
XXXXXXXXXXXXXXXXXXXXXXXXXXXXXXXXXXXXXXXXXXXXXXXX
XXXXXXXXXXXXXXXXXXXXXXXXXXXXXXXXXXXXXXXXXXXXXXXX
XXXXXXXXXXXXXXXXXXXXXXXXXXXXXXXXXXXXXXXXXXXXXXXX
XXXXXXXXXXXXXXXXXXXXXXXXXXXXXXXXXXXXXXXXXXXXXXXX
XXXXXXXXXXXXXXXXXXXXXXXXXXXXXXXXXXXXXXXXXXXXXXXX
XXXXXXXXXXXXXXXXXXXXXXXXXXXXXXXXXXXXXXXXXXXXXXXX
XXXXXXXXXXXXXXXXXXXXXXXXXXXXXXXXXXXXXXXXXXXXXXXX
XXXXXXXXXXXXXXXXXXXXXXXXXXXXXXXXXXXXXXXXXXXXXXXX
XXXXXXXXXXXXXXXXXXXXXXXXXXXXXXXXXXXXXXXXXXXXXXXX
XXXXXXXXXXXXXXXXXXXXXXXXXXXXXXXXXXXXXXXXXXXXXXXX
XXXXXXXXXXXXXXXXXXXXXXXXXXXXXXXXXXXXXXXXXXXXXXXX
XXXXXXXXXXXXXXXXXXXXXXXXXXXXXXXXXXXXXXXXXXXXXXXX
XXXXXXXXXXXXXXXXXXXXXXXXXXXXXXXXXXXXXXXXXXXXXXXX
XXXXXXXXXXXXXXXXXXXXXXXXXXXXXXXXXXXXXXXXXXXXXXXX
XXXXXXXXXXXXXXXXXXXXXXXXXXXXXXXXXXXXXXXXX I have sinned
XXXXXXXXXXXXXXXXXXXXXXXXXXXXXXXXXXXXX in that I have betrayed
XXXXXXXXXXXXXXXXXXXXXXXXXXXXXXXXXXXXXX the innocent blood.
XXXXXXXXXXXXXXXXXXXXXXXXXXXXXXXXXXXXXXXXXXXXXXXX
XXXXXXXXXXXXXXXXXXXXXXXXXXXXXXXXXXXXXXXXXXXXXXXX
XXXXXXXXXXXXXXXXXXXXXXXXXXXXXXXXXXXXXXXXXXXXXXXX

XXXXXXXXXXXXXXXXXXXXXXXXXXXXXXXXXXXXXXXXXXXXXXXXXXXX
XXXXXXXXXXXXXXXXXXXXXXXXXXXXXXXXXXXXXXXXXXXXXXXXXXXX
XXXXXXXXXXXXXXXXXXXXXXXXXXXXXXXXXXXXXXXXXXXXXXXXXXXX
XXXXXXXXXXXXXXXXXXXXXXXXXXXXXXXXXXXXXXXXXXXXXXXXXXXX
XXXXXXXXXXXXXXXXXXXXXXXXXXXXXXXXXXXXXXXXXXXXXXXXXXXX
XXXXXXXXXXXXXXXXXXXXXXXXXXXXXXXXXXXXXXXXXXXXXXXXXXXX
XXXXXXXXXXXXXXXXXXXXXXXXXXXXXXXXXXXXXXXXXXXXXXXXXXXX
XXXXXXXXXXXXXXXXXXXXXXXXXXXXXXXXXXXXXXXXXXXXXXXXXXXX
XXXXXXXXXXXXXXXXXXXXXXXXXXXXXXXXXXXXXXXXXXXXXXXXXXXX
XXXXXXXXXXXXXXXXXXXXXXXXXXXXXXXXXXXXXXXXXXXXXXXXXXXX
XXXXXXXXXXXXXXXXXXXXXXXXXXXXXXXXXXXXXXXXXXXXXXXXXXXX
XXXXXXXXXXXXXXXXXXXXXXXXXXXXXXXXXXXXXXXXXXXXXXXXXXXX
XXXXXXXXXXXXXXXXXXXXXXXXXXXXXXXXXXXXXXXXXXXXXXXXXXXX
XXXXXXXXXXXXXXXXXXXXXXXXXXXXXXXXXXXXXXXXXXXXXXXXXXXX
XXXXXXXXXXXXXXXXXXXXXXXXXXXXXXXXXXXXXXXXXXXXXXXXXXXX
XXXXXXXXXXXXXXXXXXXXXXXXXXXXXXXXXXXXXXXXXXXXXXXXXXXX
XXXXXXXXXXXXXXXXXXXXXXXXXXXXXXXXXXXXXXXXXXXXXXXXXXXX
XXXXXXXXXXXXXXXXXXXXXXXXXXXXXXXXXXXXXXXXXXXXXXXXXXXX
XXXXXXXXXXXXXXXXXXXXXXXXXXXXXXXXXXXXXXXXXXXXXXXXXXXX
XXXXXXXXXXXXXXXXXXXXXXXXXXXXXXXXXXXXXXXXXXXXXXXXXXXX
XXXXXXXXXXXXXXXXXXXXXXXXXXXXXXXXXXXXXXXXXXXXXXXXXXXX
XXXXXXXXXXXXXXXXXXXXXXXXXXXXXXXXXXXXXXXXXXXXXXXXXXXX
XXXXXXXXXXXXXXXXXXXXXXXXXXXXXXXXXXXXXXXXXXXXXXXXXXXX
XXXXXXXXXXXXXXXXXXXXXXXXXXXXXXXXXXXXXXXXXXXXXXXXXXXX
XXXXXXXXXXXXXXXXXXXXXXXXXXXXXXXXXXXXXXXXXXXXXXXXXXXX
XXXXXXXXXXXXXXXXXXXXXXXXXXXXXXXXXXXXXXXXXXXXXXXXXXXX
XXXXXXXXXXXXXXXXXXXXXXXXXXXXXXXXXXXXXXXXXXXXXXXXXXXX
XXXXXXXXXXXXXXXXXXXXXXXXXXXXXXXXXXXXXXXXXXXXXXXXXXXX
XXXXXXXXXXXXXXXXXXXXXXXXXXXXXXXXXXXXXXXXXXXXXXXXXXXX
XXXXXXXXXXXXXXXXXXXXXXXXXXXXXXXXXXXXXXXXXXXXXXXXXXXX
XXXXXXXXXXXXXXXXXXXXXXXXXXXXXXXXXXXXXXXXXXXXXXXXXXXX
XXXXXXXXXXXXXXXXXXXXXXXXXXXXXXXXXXXXXXXXXXXXXXXXXXXX
XXXXXXXXXXXXXXXXXXXXXXXXXXXXXXXXXXXXXXXXXXXXXXXXXXXX
XXXXXXXXXXXXXXXXXXXXXXXXXXXXXXXXXXXXXXXXXXXXXXXXXXXX
XXXXXXXXXXXXXXXXXXXXXXXXXXXXXXXXXXXXXXXXXXXXXXXXXXXX
XXXXXXXXXXXXXXXXXXXXXXXXXXXXXXXXXXXXXXXXXXXXXXXXXXXX
XXXXXXXXXXXXXXXXXXXXXXXXXXXXXXXXXXXXXXXXXXXXXXXXXXXX
XXXXXXXXXXXXXXXXXXXXXXXXXXXXXXXXXXXXXXXXXXXXXXXXXXXX
XXXXXXXXXXXXXXXXXXXXXXXXXXXXXXXXXXXXXXXXXXXXXXXXXXXX
XXXXXXXXXXXXXXXXXXXXXXXXXXXXXXXXXXXXXXXXXXXXXXXXXXXX
XXXXXXXXXXXXXXXXXXXXXXXXXXXXXXXXXXXXXXXXXXXXXXXXXXXX
departed XXXXXXXXXXXXXXXXXXXXXXXXXXXXXXXXXXXXXXXXXXXX
and went and hanged himself. XXXXXXXXXXXXXXXXXXXXXXXXX
XXXXXXXXXXXXXXXXXXXXXXXXXXXXXXXXXXXXXXXXXXXXXXXXXXXX
XXXXXXXXXXXXXXXXXXXXXXXXXXXXXXXXXXXXXXXXXXXXXXXXXXXX
XXXXXXXXXXXXXXXXXXXXXXXXXXXXXXXXXXXXXXXXXXXXXXXXXXXX
XXXXXXXXXXXXXXXXXXXXXXXXXXXXXXXXXXXXXXXXXXXXXXXXXXXX
XXXXXXXXXXXXXXXXXXXXXXXXXXXXXXXXXXXXXXXXXXXXXXXXXXXX
XXXXXXXXXXXXXXXXXXXXXXXXXXXXXXXXXXXXXXXXXXXXXXXXXXXX
XXXXXXXXXXXXXXXXXXXXXXXXXXXXXXXXXXXXXXXXXXXXXXXXXXXX
XXXXXXXXXXXXXXXXXXXXXXXXXXXXXXXXXXXXXXXXXXXXXXXXXXXX
XXXXXXXXXXXXXXXXXXXXXXXXXXXXXXXXXXXXXXXXXXXXXXXXXXXX
XXXXXXXXXXXXXXXXXXXXXXXXXXXXXXXXXXXXXXXXXXXXXXXXXXXX
XXXXXXXXXXXXXXXXXXXXXXXXXXXXXXXXXXXXXXXXXXXXXXXXXXXX
XXXXXXXXXXXXXXXXXXXXXXXXXXXXXXXXXXXXXXXXXXXXXXXXXXXX
XXXXXXXXXXXXXXXXXXXXXXXXXXXXXXXXXXXXXXXXXXXXXXXXXXXX
XXXXXXXXXXXXXXXXXXXXXXXXXXXXXXXXXXXXXXXXXXXXXXXXXXXX

XXXXXXX JUNE 13, 2011 XXXXXXX

XXXXXXXXXXXXXXXXXXXXXXXXXXXXXXX
XXXXXXXXXXXXXXXXXXXXXXXXXXXXXXX
XXXXXXXXXXXXXXXXXXXXXXXXXXXXXXX
XXXXXXXXXXXXX Resonating letters in red.
XX Glow in the moonlight. XXXXXXXXXX
XXXXX On a white brick wall. XXXXXXXX
XXXXXXXXXXXXXXXXXXXXXXX In an alley.
XXXXXXXXX Somewhere. XXXXXXXXXX
X My fingers are paintbrushes. XXXXXXXXXXXXX
XXXXXXXXXXXXXXXXXX A rigid, blue surrender.
XXXXXXXXXXXXXXXXXXXXXXXXXXXXXXXXXXXX
XX You cannot kill half a person. XXXXXXXXXXXXXXXXXXX
XXXXXX I know this now. XXXXXXXXXXXXXXXXXXXXXX
XXXXXXXXXXXX Devils and angels live together. XXXXXXX
XXXXXXXXXXXXXXXX Trapped inside of flesh. XXXXXXXX
XXXXXXXXXXXXXXXXXXXXXXXXXXXXXXXXXXXXXXXXXXXX
XXXXXXXXXXXXXXXXXXXXXXXXXX There is no guilt in discovery. XX
XXXXXXXXXXXXXXXXXXXXXXXXXXXXXXXXXXXXXXXXXXXX
XXXXXXXXXXXXXXXXXXXXXXXXXXXXXXXXXXXXXXXXXXXX
XXXXXXXXXXXXXXXXXXXXXXXXXXXXXXXXXXXXXXXXXXXX
XXXXXXXXXXXXXXXXXXXXXXXXXXXXXXXXXXXXXXXXXXXX
XXXXXXXXXXXXXXXXXXXXXXXXXXXXXXXXXXXXXXXXXXXX
XXXXXXXXXXXXXXXXXXXXXXXXXXXXXXXXXXXXXXXXXXXX
XXXXXXXXXXXXXXXXXXXXXXXXXXXXXXXXXXXXXXXXXXXX
XXXXXXXXXXXXXXXXXXXXXXXXXXXXXXXXXXXXXXXXXXXX
XXXXXXXXXXXXXXXXXXXXXXXXXXXXXXXXXXXXXXXXXXXX
XXXXXXXXXXXXXXXXXXXXXXXXXXXXXXXXXXXXXXXXXXXX
XXXXXXXXXXXXXXXXXXXXXXXXXXXXXXXXXXXXXXXXXXXX
XXXXXXXXXXXXXXXXXXXXXXXXXXXXXXXXXXXXXXXXXXXX

JUNE 14, 2011

He told me
he had never
felt quite so.

He told me he wanted to
spend many nights kissing
me, listening to me,
talking to me, pleasing me.

He was not the classic sort of
handsome. Far from it. No, not
my husband—my husband—far
from the grievous beauty of my
husband. But I did not want my
husband. I wanted this man.

> So very red, from his red-freckled chest to the red tangle of pubic hair that I fought through to suck him and fuck him. Loving every minute of it.

> But we did something wrong.

While I was talking to him, he dozed off, so I raised my voice a bit to get his attention, and he said, "Sorry, the conversation put me to sleep."

He gave me a penitent grin—an apology, before saying, "I'm very tired. It isn't you."

Not good enough.

I got up. Went to my purse, which sat on the hotel's dresser. Pulled out my tools—

He was smiling when I turned to face him with my hands behind my back.

I smiled in return—

A black look took hold of him—smile gone—when he observed my sawtoothed glow.

Then—

I came at him flying. Two battling knives immediately pinched him at the neck.

He flailed briefly. His memories spraying from his crumpled face through severed jugular veins. A shower upon me. His will wilting away.

136

and she shall be utterly burned with fire: for strong is the Lord God who judgeth her. And the kings of the earth, who have committed fornication and lived deliciously with her, shall bewail her, and lament for her, when they shall see the smoke of her burning, Standing afar off for the fear of her torment, saying, Alas, alas, that great city Babylon, that mighty city! for in one hour is thy judgment come. And the merchants of the earth shall weep and mourn over her; for no man buyeth their merchandise any more: The merchandise of gold, and silver, and precious stones, and of pearls, and fine linen, and purple, and silk, and scarlet, and all thyine wood, and all manner vessels of ivory, and all manner vessels of most precious wood, and of brass, and iron, and marble, And cinnamon, and odours, and ointments, and frankincense, and wine, and oil, and fine flour, and wheat, and beasts, and sheep, and horses, and chariots, and slaves, and souls of men. And the fruits that thy soul lusted after are departed from thee, and all things which were dainty and goodly are departed from thee, and thou shalt find them no more at all. The merchants of these things, which were made rich by her, shall stand afar off for the fear of her torment, weeping and wailing, And saying, Alas, alas, that great city, that was clothed in fine linen, and purple, and scarlet, and decked with gold, and precious stones, and pearls! For in one hour so great riches is come to nought. And every shipmaster, and all the company in ships, and sailors, and as many as trade by sea, stood afar off, And cried when they saw the smoke of her burning, saying, What city is like unto this great city! And they cast dust on their heads, and cried, weeping and wailing, saying, Alas, alas, that great city, wherein were made rich all that had ships in the sea by reason of her costliness! for in one hour is she made desolate. Rejoice over her, thou heaven, and ye holy apostles and prophets; for God hath avenged you on her. And a mighty angel took up a stone like a great millstone, and cast it into the sea, saying, Thus with violence shall that great city Babylon be thrown down, and shall be found no more at all. And the voice of harpers, and musicians, and of pipers, and trumpeters, shall be heard no more at all in thee; and no craftsman, of whatsoever craft he be, shall be found any more in thee; and the sound of a millstone shall be heard no more at all in thee; And the light of a candle shall shine no more at all in thee; and the voice of the bridegroom and of the bride shall be heard no more at all in thee: for thy merchants were the great men of the earth; for by thy sorceries were all nations deceived. And in her was found the blood of prophets, and of saints, and of all that were slain upon the earth. And after these things I heard a great voice of much people in heaven, saying, Alleluia; Salvation, and glory, and honour, and power, unto the Lord our God: For true and righteous are his judgments: for he hath judged the great whore, which did corrupt the earth with her fornication, and hath avenged the blood of his servants at her hand. And again they said, Alleluia. And her smoke rose up for ever and ever. And the four and twenty elders and the four beasts fell down and worshipped God that sat on the throne, saying, Amen; Alleluia. And a voice came out of the throne, saying, Praise our God, all ye his servants, and ye that fear him, both small and great. And I heard as it were the voice of a great multitude, and as the voice of many waters, and as the voice of mighty thunderings, saying, Alleluia: for the Lord God omnipotent reigneth. Let us be glad and rejoice, and give honour to him: for the marriage of the Lamb is come, and his wife hath made herself ready. And to her was granted that she should be arrayed in fine linen, clean and white: for the fine linen is the righteousness of saints. And he saith unto me, Write, Blessed are they which are called unto the marriage supper of the Lamb. And he saith unto me, These are the true sayings of God. And I fell at his feet to worship him. And he said unto me, See thou do it not: I am thy fellowservant, and of thy brethren that have the testimony of Jesus: worship God: for the testimony of Jesus is the spirit of prophecy. And I saw heaven opened, and behold a white horse; and he that sat upon him was called Faithful and True, and in righteousness he doth judge and make war. His eyes were as a flame of fire, and on his head were many crowns; and he had a name written, that no man knew, but he himself. And he was clothed with a vesture dipped in blood: and his name is called The Word of God. And the armies which were in heaven followed him upon white horses, clothed in fine linen, white and clean. And out of his mouth goeth a sharp sword, that with it he should smite the nations: and he shall rule them with a rod of iron: and he treadeth the winepress of the fierceness and wrath of Almighty God. And he hath on his vesture and on his thigh a name written, KING OF KINGS, AND LORD OF LORDS. And I saw an angel standing in the sun; and he cried with a loud voice, saying to all the fowls that fly in the midst of heaven, Come and gather yourselves together unto the supper of the great God; That ye may eat the flesh of kings, and the flesh of captains, and the flesh of mighty men, and the flesh of horses, and of them that sit on them, and the flesh of all men, both free and bond, both small and great. And I saw the beast, and the kings of the earth, and their armies, gathered together to make war against him that sat on the horse, and against his army. And the beast was taken, and with him the false prophet that wrought miracles before him, with which he deceived them that had received the mark of the beast, and them that worshipped his image. These both were cast alive into a lake of fire burning with brimstone. And the remnant were slain with the sword of him that sat upon the horse, which sword proceeded out of his mouth: and all the fowls were filled with their flesh. And I saw an angel come down from heaven, having the key of the bottomless pit and a great chain in his hand. And he laid hold on the dragon, that old serpent, which is the Devil, and Satan, and bound him a thousand years, And cast him into the bottomless pit, and shut him up, and set a seal upon him, that he should deceive the nations no more, till the thousand years should be fulfilled: and after that he must be loosed a little season. And I saw thrones, and they sat upon them, and judgment was given unto them: and I saw the souls of them that were beheaded for the witness of Jesus, and for the word of God, and which had not worshipped the beast, neither his image, neither had received his mark upon their foreheads, or in their hands; and they lived and reigned with Christ a thousand years. But the rest of the dead lived not again until the thousand years were finished. This is the first resurrection. Blessed and holy is he that hath part in the first resurrection: on such the second death hath no power, but they shall be priests of God and of Christ, and shall reign with him a thousand years. And when the thousand years are expired, **Satan shall be loosed out of his prison**, And shall go out to deceive the nations which are in the four quarters of the earth, Gog and Magog, to gather them together to battle: the number of whom is as the sand of the sea. And they went up on the breadth of the earth, and compassed the camp of the saints about, and the beloved city: and fire came down from God out of heaven, and devoured them. And the devil that deceived them was cast into the lake of fire and brimstone, where the beast and the false prophet are, and shall be tormented day and night for ever and ever. And I saw a great white throne, and him that sat on it, from whose face the earth and the heaven fled away; and there was found no place for them. And I saw the dead, small and great, stand before God; and the books were opened: and another book was opened, which is the book of life: and the dead were judged out of those things which were written in the books, according to their works. And the sea gave up the dead which were in it; and death and hell delivered up the dead which were in them: and they were judged every man according to their works. And death and hell were cast into the lake of fire. This is the second death. And whosoever was not found written in the book of life was cast into the lake of fire. And I saw a new heaven and a new earth: for the first heaven and the first earth were passed away; and there was no more sea. And I John saw the holy city, new Jerusalem, coming down from God out of heaven, prepared as a bride adorned for her husband. And I heard a great voice out of heaven saying, Behold, the tabernacle of God is with men, and he will dwell with them, and they shall be his people, and God himself shall be with them, and be their God. And God shall wipe away all tears from their eyes, and there shall be no more death, neither sorrow, nor crying, neither shall there be any more pain: for the former things are passed away. And he that sat upon the throne said, Behold, I make all things new. And he said unto me, Write: for these words are true and faithful. And he said unto me, It is done. I am Alpha and Omega, the beginning and the end. I will give unto him that is athirst of the fountain of the water of life freely. He that overcometh shall inherit all things; and I will be his God, and he shall be my son. But the fearful, and unbelieving, and the abominable, and murderers, and whoremongers, and sorcerers, and idolaters, and all liars, shall have their part in the lake which burneth with fire and brimstone: which is the second death. And there came unto me one of the seven angels which had the seven vials full of the seven last plagues, and talked with me, saying, Come hither, I will shew thee the bride, the Lamb's wife. And he carried me away in the spirit to a great and high mountain, and shewed me that great city, the holy Jerusalem, descending out of heaven from God, Having the glory of God: and her light was like unto a stone most precious, even like a jasper stone, clear as crystal; And had a wall great and high, and had twelve gates, and at the gates twelve angels, and names written thereon, which are the names of the twelve tribes of the children of Israel: On the east three gates; on the north three gates; on the south three gates; and on the west three gates. And the wall of the city had twelve foundations, and in them the names of the twelve apostles of the Lamb. And he that talked with me had a golden reed to measure the city, and the gates thereof, and the wall thereof. And the city lieth foursquare, and the length is as large as the breadth: and he measured the city with the reed, twelve thousand furlongs. The length and the breadth and the height of it are equal. And he measured the wall thereof, an hundred and forty and four cubits, according to the measure of a man, that is, of the angel. And the building of the wall of it was of jasper: and the city was pure gold, like unto clear glass. And the foundations of the wall of the city were garnished with all manner of precious stones. The first foundation was jasper; the second, sapphire; the third, a chalcedony; the fourth, an emerald; The fifth, sardonyx; the sixth, sardius; the seventh, chrysolite; the eighth, beryl; the ninth, a topaz; the tenth, a chrysoprasus; the eleventh, a jacinth; the twelfth, an amethyst. And the twelve gates were twelve pearls; every several gate was of one pearl: and the street of the city was pure gold, as it were transparent glass. And I saw no temple therein: for the Lord God Almighty and the Lamb are the temple of it. And the city had no need of the sun, neither of the moon, to shine in it: for the glory of God did lighten it, and the Lamb is the light thereof. And the nations of them which are saved shall walk in the light of it: and the kings of the earth do bring their glory and honour into it. And the gates of it shall not be shut at all by day: for there shall be no night there. And they shall bring the glory and honour of the nations into it. And there shall in no wise enter into it any thing that defileth, neither whatsoever worketh abomination, or maketh a lie: but they which are written in the Lamb's book of life. And he shewed me a pure river of water of life, clear as crystal, proceeding out of the throne of God and of the Lamb. In the midst of the street of it, and on either side of the river, was there the tree of life, which bare twelve manner of fruits, and yielded her fruit every month: and the leaves of the tree were for the healing of the nations. And there shall be no more curse: but the throne of God and of the Lamb shall be in it; and his servants shall serve him: And they shall see his face; and his name shall be in their foreheads. And there shall be no night there; and they need no candle, neither light of the sun; for the Lord God giveth them light: and they shall reign for ever and ever. And he said unto me, These sayings are faithful and true: and the Lord God of the holy prophets sent his angel to shew unto his servants the things which must shortly be done. Behold, I come quickly: blessed is he that keepeth the sayings of the prophecy of this book. And I John saw these things, and heard them. And when I had heard and seen, I fell down to worship before the feet of the angel which shewed me these things. Then saith he unto me, See thou do it not: for I am thy fellowservant, and of thy brethren the prophets, and of them which keep the sayings of this book: worship God. And he saith unto me, Seal not the sayings of the prophecy of this book: for the time is at hand. He that is unjust, let him be unjust still: and he which is filthy, let him be filthy still: and he that is righteous, let him be righteous still: and he that is holy, let him be holy still. And, behold, I come quickly; and my reward is with me, to give every man according as his work shall be. I am Alpha and Omega, the beginning and the end, the first and the last. Blessed are they that do his commandments, that they may have right to the tree of life, and may enter in through the gates into the city. For without are dogs, and sorcerers, and whoremongers, and murderers, and idolaters, and whosoever loveth and maketh a lie. I Jesus have sent mine angel to testify unto you these things in the churches. I am the root and the offspring of David, and the bright and morning star. And the Spirit and the bride say, Come. And let him that heareth say, Come. And let him that is athirst come. And whosoever will, let him take the water of life freely. For I testify unto every man that heareth the words of the prophecy of this book, If any man shall add unto these things, God shall add unto him the plagues that are written in this book: And if any man shall take away from the words of the book of this prophecy, God shall take away his part out of the book of life, and out of the holy city, and from the things which are written in this book. He which testifieth these things saith, Surely I come quickly. Amen. Even so, come, Lord Jesus.

JUNE 15, 2011

Ecclesiastes 9

1 For all this I considered in my heart even to declare all this, that the righteous, and the wise, and their works, are in the hand of God: no man knoweth either love or hatred by all that is before them. 2 All things come alike to all: there is one event to the righteous, and to the wicked; to the good and to the clean, and to the unclean; to him that sacrificeth, and to him that sacrificeth not: as is the good, so is the sinner; and he that sweareth, as he that feareth an oath. 3 This is an evil among all things that are done under the sun, that there is one event unto all: yea, also the heart of the sons of men is full of evil, and madness is in their heart while they live, and after that they go to the dead.

* * *

I wonder if humans are only multifunctional manipulators with factory automation and specialized devices. I wonder if God created humans for entertainment purposes only. I wonder if God likes a good thriller. Humans enjoy murder and mayhem. Humans exploit murder and mayhem. Is God any different? Is Earth's frontier a canvas in which spontaneous art is created? Are humans an installation piece? How long does it takes for a chemical explosion to turn into intellectual chaos? How long does it take amoebas to turn into David Berkowitz?

I am doing the work of God. For God. With God. As a child of God. And rest assured, God loves every minute of the madness I have created.

JUNE 16, 2011

I leave her bruised around her neck
and   after
ever   are
som   look
she

She   is a
beat   ghtly
dera   a lot
like me, except I cheer for no one.

Proceed to the next sacrifice. The next sacrifice. The next sacrifice. The next sacrifice. The next sacrifice. The next sacrifice. The next sacrifice. The next sacrifice. The next sacrifice. The next sacrifice. The next sacrifice. The next sacrifice. The next sacrifice. The next sacrifice. The next sacrifice. The next sacrifice.

JUNE 17, 2011

Mid-night. Cold. Your nipples are hard. A butterfly knife is in your pocket.

You wipe blood off your face so you can see to walk. Walk in circles.

These days the sunset and the sunrise are no different. You find balance in this.

JUNE 18, 2011

She was only sixteen. She was. She was running from a problematic situation and ran into a terrible enigma—I do know. I am not completely handicapped by my disease.

She could not have been more wrong when she decided that me getting her a hotel room was the nicest thing that anyone has ever done for her.

It takes maybe three beers to get a sixteen-year-old buzzing. It takes six to get her pants off and have her on top of you. It takes ten beers laced with Ambien for a sixteen-year-old to not realize that her eyes have been plucked from her head.

A demon escaped through her base chakra as her heart collapsed under the weight of my pounding fist. The demon ascended in a flash. Poof it was gone.

My hissing gave me goose bumps.

JUNE 19, 2011

I drive through a neighborhood in a tied up woman's minivan.

I am clean. I am beautiful. I protrude in a crowd.

People do say … my glow has returned.

I have an address in my hand. I find the house it matches. It clicks: the girl on the bus.

I follow her car. She enters a restaurant. I watch her from a bench outside of the café. She is sitting right in front of me, maybe ten feet away, but glass stands between us.

I put my fingers down my throat until I gag.

I want her.

No.

I throw up bile and acid.

My stomach cramps.

I continue to gag myself. Blood on my fingertips. Blood in my bile.

I need her.

My stomach churns with life. A stirring inside of me that compels me—dragoons me: a loaded carbine breathing fire and propelling projectiles into my core—to feed it spirits from the external world.

Who will quench its appetite today? Will this one have a face? Because I do not remember any faces right now. I only remember parts of torsos, limbs and organs.

JUNE 20, 2011

One loves—to hate—to love.

JUNE 21, 2011

I did not realize the size of it all. I am a star.

JUNE 23, 2011

I am on the edge of a bed. There is no white left on the bed sheet.

My ribs. How they protrude.

JULY 3, 2011

I set out on a course.

I found keys in my pocket and they took me to a car. I got into the car. A heart is in the glove box; it is the heart of a girl who I met on a bus, it is a heart taken from a body that I left behind. It is my nourishment, and so far it is not beating an endless beat in my head. It is only an object that came from an object that occupied a point on another object that floats in a galaxy full of objects. Even space is an object, just another thing that is manipulated by the hands of man—something to bend for our pleasure. Bend like all of the flesh-and-blood objects I have manipulated and consumed. Everyone plays a part in the manipulation of every single object to its eventual decline.

* * *

The baby needs me.

JULY 4, 2011

I pull into a gas station and while my tank fills, I run across the road to a liquor store. A pair of teens confronts me as I enter the shop, delivering worn out expressions regarding my sexuality that read as a satire, a parodic glance at the age of youth. The store's clerk eyes the teens as they roam the aisles, looking over a magazine designed for his filthy mind. He puffs a cigarette that dangles from his lips, and smoke climbs over his nostrils and continues up his slanted head past a wincing eye. He is beaten. The teens giggle—high. Maroon, hooded jackets hang from their slumped but happy shoulders. They push each other as they stroll, bumping into the store's racks.

As they fumble down an aisle, one wrestles the other into a metal stand of vodka. Bottles shake and rattle, and the station agent is now heavily fixed upon them. His neck is slung out as his cigarette butt burns; it is barely attached to his tacky lips.

"Hey," he says.

The kids immediately say in unison: "Fuck you."

"Get the fuck out of here," he gently persuades, and it really is gentle, the guy is barely alive.

"They're with me," I say, "but they'll wait outside."

He nods. I nod. The teens nod with a confounded but rather pleased look about themselves as I hold up a twelve pack of beer in one hand and point to the door with it; a bottle of Johnnie Walker pulls at me from the other hand. The kids move to the front of the store, both of them dragging through and past me.

I buy. I leave. I talk. The kids follow.

There is a small window open in my shitty hotel room, and a cloud of dust from the dirt parking lot kicks up and passes through the screen. I cough—

Thirteen empty bottles are scattered among a dazzling display of limbs and purple skin. I am counting teeth, making sure I have them all before I get into a car and drive away.

I hum a song that I do not know as I take a ramp onto a highway. Fireworks claw through the sky in front of me, fading, clawing, fading, clawing.

MASQUE

JULY 5, 2011

The masque emerged because of the need to disguise. One is someone else within a masque. There is freedom. There is representation and misrepresentation. There is anonymity. There is an outlet. Obscurity is the destination. The masque alleviates guilt.

The masque gives license. There is role-play, and role-playing is a formidable way to reach people. It brings out desire.

People are hypnotized by the masque. And then hypnotized further into freely masquerading.

The masque of red death surrounds me, but I am not death itself. I am not even an agent of Red Death. Like the others I would prefer to be considered a victim of the hideous pestilence.

But someone has to live to tell the tale, and I happen to be this story's narrator.

The masque of red death plunges mortals into immortality. There is a buzz. There is surprise. There is terror and horror. There is disgust. Darkness and decay hold eventual dominion.

I am here and I am there. I am anachronistic. I have survived the past. I fight through the present. I know my future.

JULY 6, 2011

I am trying to do science here. I am trying to draw a response. I collect data in order to find out what affects you.

KIDNAPPING

JULY 7, 2011

A psychologist once told me that I am untreatable. She said that the drugs to treat one mental ailment compound the intensity of the other mental ailments. But to me she was saying, "You're fucked. Deal with it." I was twelve.

I do the best I can.

JULY 8, 2011

There is a car in the driveway. It is the same BMW that I keyed what seems so long ago. The key mark is still there. The light that is above the garage is activated by my movement. But it goes off and on all the time. The resident of this home would not be startled by it, but an intruder is supposed to be. This intruder is not. This intruder is scared of nothing.

The key I hold does not work. Of course the locks have been changed. I wait down the street, resting in a neighbor's grass. The garbage truck rambles down the road. It is 6 a.m.

My life in words describes different angles of a conceptual world that "defines" violence and sexual deviance. And yet I have faith and trust in the static world—the contours of my back nestled into rigid green blades of grass—the revolving, schedule-oriented world, a world etched in stone that rarely changes even as chaos hovers above it. Alarm clocks ring, people shit and shave, people put on their uniforms and punch clocks. Everything rhymes in this neighborhood. Except me.

How am I here? On a street with one million dollar homes. How did I end up here? On this street. Before. Now.

JULY 9, 2011

A U2 CD gave me a twenty-two-year-old song. "Running to Stand Still". I remember when you used to play it on a loop as you went to sleep, almost seven years ago when we met. It did not mean anything to me then. It was just a lullaby. It means everything now.

I pushed a button on the stereo and the CD turned. It was right there and ready to go. I just needed some noise while killing time after breaking into your house and looking through old photo albums, but the song gave me so much more than noise. Hurt. Fear. Guilt. Anger. Why do you have the song ready to go at this point in time? Are you playing it for me? Or your new love? I'm confused.

I cannot remember now if it is you or me who suffers from the needle chill. But I do know that nothing is conventional.

"… she runs through the streets
With her eyes painted red
Under black belly of cloud in the rain
In through a doorway she brings me
White gold and pearls stolen from the sea
She is raging
She is raging and the storm blows up in her eyes
She will suffer the needle chill
She is running to stand still …"

JULY 10, 2011

I hide in the dark of a closet until the time is right. I steal a life from a crib.

MEXICO

JULY 11, 2011

i cross the border into mexico without a hitch
into a shitty border town and i am driving and
my baby girl is screaming and we are both
hungry and our mouths are dry and she finally
falls asleep like a coma after what seems like
hours of high pitched heartache i stop for gas
and some cerveza and i drink and sweat and
drive and my head is a mess of hammers hitting
and the baby is screaming she hasnt eaten in a
day and she doesnt like the taste of beer so she
falls into a death coma again i wake her and her
eyes limply raise to recognition and her chin
falls to her chest when she tries to look into her
mommys eyes she laps water from a water
bottle but most of the liquid falls on her shirt
and she is still strapped into her car seat and
she reaches for me but i have to drive and she

sucks the water out of her shirt the best she can
and passes out again

JULY 12, 2011

The sea spins energy, rushing forward and chasing your tiny toes. Spilling giggles and bringing you gifts. Shells and rocks are diamonds in your eyes.

The sun arcs and shadows fall through bold eyelashes, caressing blush cheeks. And a smile of wonder arranged by a seagull overtakes you. That smile is the only thing I find authentic. That smile is my destination.

Healthy notions take me. Inspiration. Liberty. Optimism that is real and substantial. There is so much joy in coming and going with you.

Beautiful baby girl.

JULY 14, 2011

My disposition was shaped when I was five, six and seven. Ferocious physical abuse. Punches. Broken bones. Skin punctured and stitched. My disposition was shaped from eighteen to twenty-one. A cult and ritual rape by several men at once, all the time. Dropped in a world of malaise. Crackling and wheezing sound. I was left for dead. Removed from my condition because I became a useless cavity. Deranged and suffering. Swallowed by shock therapy, solitary confinement, and lithium in the hopes that my long-term memory might be erased.

RETURN

JULY 16, 2011

I put the baby in a carriage. I set the carriage on my husband's porch. I leave her behind, so I can go feed demons.

NOVEMBER 24, 2011

NOVEMBER 28, 2011

I am in a room. Candles. Red chairs.

I spot a victim. Someone torn. Someone in a trap and attempting to gnaw at his leg to free himself. I know he is torn and trapped because he is the only one not handcuffed to a conversation (other than me) in the bar where we reside. He does not mingle. He is not examining the reproductive properties of the opposite sex. Instead, this man taps keys on his laptop at a bar, paying attention to no one. Who does that? Totally consumed by something upsetting. He writes.

I will free him from his peril.

"Company?"

He looks up for a second and says, "No, thanks." Drops his head. Returns to typing.

Not as easy as I thought.

"Why not? You shouldn't be sitting alone," I say.

"I prefer to sit alone."

He continues to type, but begins to miss the correct keys. Delete, delete. Type, type. A challenge. But still torn. He is disturbed. I can break him. Take him.

"Is there something about me that you find suspect? I'm a little hurt."

He stops. Looks up. He grabs the back of his neck with one hand and massages it a bit. Sighs. Gives me an anxious look. Says—

"You're not doing me a favor by releasing me from loneliness. As I said, I prefer to sit alone."

He leans back, takes in all of me, and gives a weak smile.

"You've got blood on your hands," he says.

"Oh, do I?"

"Yes."

He chews on his thumbnail as he observes me with an egregious grin. I take a seat across from him.

"It's been rough lately," I say.

"I know."

"And how do you know?"

"It is written."

"What do you mean?"

"It's all over you."

"I see. Why are you in a bar with a computer?"

"To drink, to observe, to take notes. To be in the atmosphere of my subject matter."

"What is your subject matter?"

"Currently? YOU."

"Really? And what else?"

"Failure. The death of our species."

"Interesting. You're a sociologist."

"I suppose." He pauses. There is an awkward moment of no words as we stare at each other with ownership of one another. "I also have blood on my hands."

He is opening up to me.

"Do you?" I ask.

"I'm a marked man."

He tells me that he has just recently published a book, and the book created an uprising in the small community of Celina, Texas, where he taught high school English. He was banished.

"I corrupt young minds," he continues. "I steal innocence. My work is pornographic, sacrilegious, and graphically violent. Or so they say."

We talk for about fifteen minutes about his scattered, bohemian life, and then he tells me he must go, and I understand that I am going to lose him if I'm not careful.

"Come to my hotel," I say.

"Come to my house," he says.

I do.

I enter his home and it smells of rust. Newspapers cover the windows. Minimally furnished. Framed Salvador Dali prints are the only decoration—grotesque drawings.

I have a seat on his couch while he takes a phone call in the other room. His book sits on a feeble end table: *With Deepest Regrets*. I pick it up and begin reading—

I am immediately sucked into his memoir, a cruel book within a cruel world, a cruel world that sounds too familiar.

And then I find myself in his book.

Literally find myself—

Truly find myself—

In Chapter 08.

In Chapter 08 of the book he speaks of a "beaten and bruised and slightly deranged cheerleader" he once knew in high school.

I am that cheerleader.

"Robin?"

No answer.

I continue to read—the sun comes up—all the way to the end. I am in a fog because I am connected to this story, this chaotic story that thoroughly confuses me and has no end. And now I sit inside of his red house. A red house that did not exist until his book was published.

I sit back. Terror creeps.

"Robin!"

No answer.

This book. This terrible book. It is within this appalling book and inside of his dirty words that I am marked forever? I am now forever attached to this unrefined memoir? This book that needs a thorough editing. This book missing in important details all the way through. This book put together by what is clearly a novice author. This book with an unfocused plot and a stagnant ending—it sits in waters that haven't moved in years. This disaster of prose!

This uncomfortable book that owns none of its own despair. This book that blames others for his faulty existence. Blames me as well, it seems.

The devil just wants to kill you, Robin, and sadly, I think you are letting It!

And it is with this spitting thought that the house takes hold of me. It is not happy for I have upset its black heart—

There is a bit of a chill in the air. The gas heater shoots a flame and then the heater's slow motor begins to cycle, maneuvers, growling out a semi-warm blow of air.

There are dust particles falling all around me. I see them clearly in the low light of the morning sun that causes each speck to shine like something spectacular, diamond dust, but far from it. The dust from the vent flows into the already descending particles, and my lungs pull them into my mouth and nose as I breath. Dead skin drifting about along with refractory pieces of pre-solar stars. What else is in the air?

I don't know. Lots of things in the old crimson house I now occupy—

There is never anything good to be found in the history of an old house or the past inhabitants would still be living in it; something better came along or something evil pushed the past owners out. In many ways, this old house was abandoned, several times I'm sure, and I am breathing in the many reasons.

Then—

I cannot move and my thoughts are seized and removed by force.

Drip, drip all around.

The red light from the DVD player strangles me, and the blanket that sits on a bench across the room looks as if it has been tampered with—the shape of someone is upon it and then the shape is gone. The particles of dust grow frenetically busy, circling, following some force, flowing sideways.

Something brushes against me.

The air around me expands, and something inside of me is like a plant growing in an awkward way in order to get the most sunlight. Something inside of me is like a growing tree that decides that it's easier to become one with the object in its way instead of maneuver around it, splitting itself through, grafting, fusing. I am like a vine that paints the siding of a house with flaring leaves and intricate designs of disillusioned stems—I look pretty, but in the end I am nothing more than an array of leaf-shaped termites, creating dysfunction and decay and weakening the home.

I am a woman who surrenders to rape—again and again—and then is raped while her husband watches, gets pregnant, delivers a baby, a baby who wears the woman's abuse everyday, a baby who grows up and rapes in retaliation for her pain.

This was me, following a trail of parting dust into the bedroom, and allowing the ceiling to crash down upon me like razor-sharp hail, and the walls to heave inward with its horrible, decorative texture of gut-colored inch worms, getting larger and closer and covering me, attempting to destroy me.

I run into the closet. I close the door and have a seat, and call—

"Robin!"

But the only thing I hear in return is a cat's murmur, somewhere around me, dense and isolated, hyperventilating. The light from the bottom of the door disappears, the doorknob is gone, the box around me is fast approaching, and it is hot, sizzling against me in all of my nakedness, burrowing into my skin. Spikes that have motion, rotating like a corkscrew into my flesh.

I call for Robin again, but a cat whimpering is still the return. The sound of the cat is loose upon me, and absorbed immediately, so it must be close. It is all around, it is not an echo; no, because, again, it is near me, maybe inside of me. We are all connected now, the space of the closet, the dissected cat, a flowing murmur, and the mountain of dust particles that flow into my lungs and consume me.

And then I hear a voice—not mine—calming the cat and its whimper is gone.

But still—

DECEMBER 6, 2011

I was born in Saint-Trond. I was orphaned at the age of fifteen. I spent my days lying in fields of open grass, getting closer to God. My oath to the Lord was a conviction that forced me to neglect my physical body. I went days, then weeks, then months without eating. I went into shock, I had a seizure, I died. While the priest informed my family and friends about my righteous virtue, I soared out of my coffin until I reached the rafters of the cathedral. I stood, knees bent, perched upon a beam like a bird, attempting to escape the smell of human evil.

During my coma I visited Hell, Purgatory, and then I landed at the feet of God. I kneeled before It, and It stroked my hair. It offered me a choice: I could enter the gates of Heaven or return to Earth to suffer. If I returned to Earth, my suffering would release the dwellers of Purgatory, so I came back to live among the mortals, to live among the damned. I returned to live in the trees, perched on tiny branches among nature's creatures, living off my own breasts' milk.

DECEMBER 9, 2011

It certainly is not a flattering pose. I suppose it could be if it did not appear suspended. Because it is not. In reality the pose is part of a shift and rotation. But the position is still compromising because the shift is so very slow. The rotation is not even visible unless you notice subtle movements. So to most, the position in space appears to be nothing but a disastrous installation piece, direct, and without substance. The worst kind.

DECEMBER 10, 2011

I get up from the curb.

A train, faint in the distance, sticks to the air and soaks up the sound of the evening.

The night is chilly. No wind.

The moon is a bursting hole I desire to be vacuumed through. Oh, take me, release me, moon. I focus into its pockmarks. Tides rise and fall, rocks die, grinding into sand. Sand climbs from the water, and like bits of glass, challenges and sheers opposing blades of grass. Plants are uprooted and trees are blasted of their bark and robbed of their leaves.

Roads connect. Ys and Ts and Xes. Triangles on squares. Lines waver into porous metal.

Cotton curls. Red liquid flows and hemorrhages, and then coagulates and heals.

The brace of a scab. New skin outlined by the old.

Original sin all around the fringe.

I pass two familiar vehicles and then break the glass on the front door of my husband's home. I put my hand through the window and unlock the door.

My husband has just finished fucking my friend. They are cleaning off the decay from their unsanitary spots. I scuffle with the intruder while my husband calls 9-1-1. I am hitting the intruder over and over with a closed fist. She lies on the floor in a ball, covering her head.

My husband grabs my leg and drags me off of the bed. I look over at the smoldering television to see myself on a liquor store surveillance video.

"If you know this woman contact …"

My husband continues to drag me through the house. I hear a police siren. I kick my foot free. I hop to my feet.

I am standing several paces from the man who murdered me in Galveston. I am facing him. He is breathing heavily. He takes a step in my direction.

"Oh, how I'd like to melt your bones, you fucker," I snarl.

He stops in his tracks.

"You're sick," he returns.

Sirens get closer.

I run out the backdoor.

Cities just appear and then disappear. Butterflies, swooping, smacking. Speed limits change, but my speed remains the same. Red lights in small towns are not regarded. I'm almost out of gas. A cop is ten feet behind the car I am driving. Another one arrives. And another.

I panic. I am unsure of who I am—on a trip through strange corridors—or what I could have done.

I pull the car to a stop. And RUN. I never look back as I dart through knee-high vegetation to a dark stretch of woods. Howling as I go.

SHADOWS

DECEMBER 25, 2011

JANUARY 1, 2012

JANUARY 10, 2012

My loins were injected with a demon child by a team of rapists nineteen months ago.

JANUARY 11, 2012

Shadows are matter.
are the sUNRISE.
are a MEmory.
and the nEXt.
are the missing MEmories.
are we—MISSing?

Shadows are. around me. on me. of me.

The lies off the watershed,

the gaping hole,

the fantasy.

JANUARY 12, 2012

Tranquility brushes a coat of gloss across the gray. It shines outward into the beating heart of existence and spreads out like a cloak and hood that hides a ferocious fiend. The light from our passing of the sun reveals a smile that delivers with sincerity. My lips are pink and popping with a thirst for blood, a desire that drips into a pool of water and casts like the ripples from a stone's throw to a cluster of sharks that eat their own tails in a frenzy.

Lick the sugar of your lust until you swell. Beast. Contemptuous beast. Gluttonous, overexposed animal that you are.

JANUARY 13, 2012

There is an uprising stuck in the breezes of my sternum. I am ready to go.

In my waning days, I am struck.

A heaven takes form.

This heaven is only rest.

My mind's matter is retained within a bridge of no definition.

A soul with no body to attach itself descends into an effervescent sleep.

There is no suffering, and I am well-acquainted with suffering.

To those still daunted by the pleasure of sustained rest: unlock the creator, and with faith find a way for him to escape into your heart.

Unlock the throat he spirals through; it is parallel to your own.

Through all my thoughts and visions, I have never found a way to release the creator and bring him home to me. Maybe someone will help. Perchance, someone will rewrite my destiny.

January 22, 2012

We met in the menacing cloud of a war. A beast that shifted in the fore of a pale blue atmosphere.

On that day. Everyday.

Nothing more than an eyesore.

There was nothing to gain in fate. Flat was fate—pressed and pat. A frenzied fire that fell upon us in the flow of feet marching and fists poking into the air of the furrowed brow that fed our intellect.

We held hands—intertwined fingers locked into one another— smothered by his grip so tight and tense.

His fingers were dry, his knuckles scarred, his imprint hypnotizing in the elegance of the design, like twine, unrolled into the sea, grabbed by a hurricane and spun into something new, dynamic, and full of energy, never settling.

It rained that day. The drops were acid, falling into puddles of oil on the asphalt road. The mixture of acid and oil borrowed from the colors of a rainbow, but there was no beauty in the mix because darkness was chasing it into a hole. Inside the hole, the colors could not hold form, and after a time, they completely lost their essence—their vivid detail—and washed away in the dense undercoat of gloom.

He was strong, angry, enlightened, and the shade of his skin was the base of his existence. His life was owned by no one, but it was sacrificed for us all.

I was a reflection of all the cruelty of the world. There was no luster inside of me. There was no life inside of me. There were only images of serrated edges, nooses, and shallow graves.

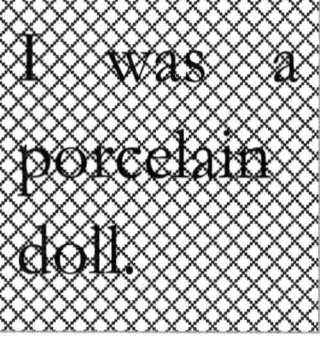

Imbedded outward of me were only those things.

My God was immature. **My God** chose sides and decided the fate of conflicts according to who praised and worshipped him more. **My God** did not care about sacrifice unless the sacrifice was to set aside time to outwardly sing praises to Him. **My God** was still a Him, and not an It or a She.

We devoted ritual ceremonies to our Savior, and **my God** enjoyed the sacraments and the flicker of the flame—His cross captured in gasoline and broken into pieces, hissing, the wind tearing it into something new, ash ascending into the sky aboard a machine oiled by degeneration as we hid behind our pride in white masques of red death.

The river ran shallow, but it still bored a hole through my home, and I was constantly swimming to keep from drowning, never understanding that my bent knees could extend and touch the bottom.

"How much blood?"

The blood was black. Mostly smeared across his face and soaking into his hair. The blood also dripped across the collar of his jacket, a funnel for the rest of his coat, which was now soaked through and heavy.

The mark of blood on his forehead was the imprint of a ship that followed a triangle. There was a language on the vessel, but the people who spoke it were already dead, so communication was missing except for one prayer that evaporated into space, reaching no one.

"There is no blood."

He seemed confused, but he smiled. And then he presented me with a wish. He put the wish in my hand and closed it from view one finger at a time. When his eyelids dropped for a long, subdued blink, a blink so long it broke into the submissive world of the dead, I made my wish.

His eyes opened—the wish was already doing its job. Life coursed through him just as violence grabbed me from behind. I was raised to my feet and pulled, dragging, to a scaffold. Fists raged, pounding into me. My nose became a spiral and my eyes sank deep beneath raised flesh. My teeth were shattered, every one, busting through my lips. My hearing went to a stream of an alarm sounding a storm, and after a few minutes, there was no noise except the echo of hammering feet against me. Cracked ribs became punctured lungs. Compound fractures became holes through my skin that emptied

The nothing became something and that something became a piercing blue facade connected to the rest of a horizon. The horizon was mellow and so were the differing shapes of me.

blood and eventually light, and then past light to darkness, to nothing.

I became a free-form floating, fasting myself to a flame and dangling in the denseness of my own dying force before I advanced by way of a cloud drift into a beautiful grassland, settling into the dirt, becoming dirt itself. My nutrients aroused a people, feet running and standing still, earth unfurled and sowed, creating the properties in life everywhere.

Imagine the erosion of a rock. It breaks into pieces, finds a stream, tumbles into an ocean, and rolls back and forth until it is the sediment at the base of a continent where travelers go to feast on the sun. Those specks of sand began as a piece of crust—noble was that slice of imbedded earth. That imbedded earth was once a prism of light, and before that, it was a loop of darkness, and before it was a loop, it was a parallel line to a parallel structure.

The rain was a solid sheet, hit by a block of interconnected kinetic energies, laying everything to waste. The rain never stopped. It fell until its waters pushed past the Kármán line, evacuating dead bodies into space. The bodies became fuel for the energy of a god, who destroyed life instead of creating and nurturing it.

That piece of crust died in a rainstorm one million years ago.

I was all of those things and more, and now I am a stalk that grows into the nutrients of you.

I took the train to the station, the days in my hometown finished. Diminished. Dated. I hated to leave my mother, sister and brother. I hated to head across several towns and smother the existence of another, the man of my wretched dreams.

The strobe straddled the bench where I was sitting, finding my one green eye and then the other. I am told my eyes are brilliant, but I have never looked to see.

I don't remember how I ended up in that particular spot, captured by a dismal stretch of music, alone, filled with inebriation, concocted lies and alibis. Settled, situated, barbiturate-aided, traded, long-pained and alienated from those who elevated me into the drab, red fury of lights flashing, dancing, dying.

I used to have such a masterful shroud inside the bewitched bathing pool of my mind.

Already developed within me was the way he carried himself—

His molasses drawl was already attached to his lanky bones. Thin bones that carried from his toes to his hips to his lips. Intoxicating thin lips. Lips that smacked, bones that rattled, and all bound by sugar beets that dripped like a mudslide into my mouth, into my mind, settling there.

I wanted to pass existence in his words. I wanted him to fill me up with his selfish intentions because he came to me from a fold inside my brain before I was even born.

My dream of him brought me to an unopened door, to the other side of him, where he strangled me, leaving me underwater for a time, as he cavorted into my submissiveness.

My dream of him brought me to an unopened door, to the other side of him, where he strangled me, leaving me underwater for a time, as he cavorted into my submissiveness.

I followed him. He was not a leader, he did not know how to lead, he did not want to lead, he was not even leading, and yet I followed. I followed, flowing into a molasses stream that bowed to the throws of a universal sickness.

I will tell you the story but as I saw it in my dream; it includes the richness of his culture, his iconic upbringing in his mass of tall and thin, but more expansive in substance, and closer to

"Hold it a fashion and a toy in blood; A violet in the youth of primy nature. Forward, not permanent, sweet, not lasting. The perfume and suppliance of a minute— No more."

the hypnotizing verse of the loop in my mind, closer to Hamlet, and the trifling of his favor.

He would say:

"WE will split the sea, and WE will be on this side—tied to a mast—OUR ears covered as to not hear the song of progress. OUR wish is to revert back to the days when it was OK to divide with cultural pride, when knights fought, knowing they would die for the regression of war."

I nodded my head. I response because I his ideas—I had in my life, and the received all turned

never returned a was mesmerized by received few words scarce words I had into ritual rape—

The gallery that day was rich with color. I recall white lights watching the re-creation of life through the happiness found in Christians battling.

There was also the moon standing on a wave and opening up the sky to the tension of seagulls drifting into crystal zoological gardens where animals wept in a dust cloud of their own sweat.

Out of that garden stepped a man with two ankhs tightly bound in his fists. His beard was an Egyptian slip from the 12th dynasty. He came after me upon the completion of a murder—his father—while fighting a war in a distant property. He spent thirty years as a king, and yet he came at me like a dog, his natural state. The eventide's stars promoted him after a series of trials as a black hole inside of a black hole, drifting in the illusion of a boy's reoccurring dream. The boy who was in a coma resisted the temptation to wake because that dream was the boy's life. It was his existence. The shell of that dream was tapped into unnatural devices and prayers to false idols, which were connected to a plane of parasites that dipped into their capital and used it to spill blood.

The reoccurring dream started to fade

Psalms 137

9 Happy shall he be, that taketh and dasheth thy little ones against the stones.

after several centuries, forming a line into the realm of a more deserving void of space, before becoming the energy of a walking famine that was evoked by a nomarch who dwelled in a tomb. The energy from that deceased nomarch eventually escaped into me.

2 Kings 2

23 And he went up from thence unto Bethel: and as he was going up by the way, the "Are you sure that you want to paint your eyes like a cat?" I asked. nd mocked him, and said unto him, Go up, thou bald head; go up, thou bald head.

24 And he turned back, and looked on them, and cursed the "Are you sure that you want to paint your eyes like a cat?" I asked. he LO me forth two she bears out of the wood, and tare forty and two children of them.

He pulled my blouse up over my arms as my skirt fell into the coil of a snake that struck and temporarily paralyzed me. I wished for him to pierce me with his silver staff, and as I waited for his arrival to my south, he appeared to my north. and his I inhaled, intrusion stretched into me. I went many seconds without a breath and then a million souls turned to dust. Sperm, the trained robbers of the egg, have no home when they arrive in purgatory, after being wasted on rape.

> Ezekiel 23
>
> 19 Yet she multiplied her whoredoms, in calling to remembrance the days of her youth, wherein she had played the harlot in the land of Egypt. 20 For she doted upon their paramours, whose flesh is as the flesh of asses, and whose issue is like the issue of horses.

He laughed at me, tied me up, and put me in his closet. I waited there for days, wasting away. The molecules of air that entered me while in the closet were once a part of a complex solar system until a star in the system ran out of hydrogen at its core, engulfing the planets in its vicinity. Those smothered planets broke into pieces and became the humidity around me after losing their way during a conquest in a desert land. That old and wise interpretation of moisture created slack in the rope that held me, and I pulled out a hand and I killed with it. I took a hammer and smashed it into what eventually became a molecule in a bed of ice beneath the surface of a planetoid that had yet to form.

I sat there in a river of blood, treading for some time before leaving, and then I swiftly trekked across hot asphalt in the middle of the night until I arrived at a volcano. I sat beside the hole that a lava flow had hollowed out while saying a few prayers, and I then jumped into the abyss. While I was falling, I dreamed of a man, and then met him, a lanky link of a mortal who pulled me into a molasses river, then pushed me into a freedom march, two sides fighting for the empowerment of their people in much the same way, but very different.

However, before I met him, I was still falling. I fell for days until I realized that I was not a person falling; I was the fall itself, for my person had already been consumed by a molten fire's very subtle and soft touch.

It is hard to make a difference in this world when you are a particle in a molten landscape, but I did eventually make an impact when I helped cover a town with a flowing fire so deep that nothing survived.

Many years later, I caught the eye of an archeologist, who was excavating the area where the volcano had spilled. A dash of energy created by a glance toward me floating by him, sent a shock that pushed me through

And for that hour of discovery, and for evermore, I was linked to Heracles, the son of Zeus and Queen Alcmene of Thebes.

a small whirlwind, which triggered a linguist on the site to ponder the origin of the word "Vesuvius".

Many writers refer to Zeus as Hués because of

the sector
soul that
the rains
and
Heracles
called
huios or
Zeus". The
who saw the
realized that
transliterate
"V", which
normal state
and you also
the other
"V" instead
"HY", and
the Latin

of his lost
controlled
and dews,
therefore
was often
Huésou
"son of
linguist,
dust of me,
if you
the "ou" as
is the
of affairs,
transliterate
upsilons as
of the usual
you change
normative

ending "us", it forms VESVVIVS or Vesuvius.

> That thought remained and so did I because I became that thought, connecting to the tissue of his brain and finding a home, long after he had moved onto translations in other areas of interest.

> When he died, so did the few cells I occupied, and therefore I moved forward as well, into space, becoming a sound wave that caught the attention of a short wave radio operator, who thought he had heard an extraterrestrial crying, and he was right.

I then became a fluff of organic material that was utilized to create a piece of thread, and that filament was used to create a dynamic partition between two colliding spiral universes. When the experiment broke down to nothing, I became the curving, dusty arm of a pinwheel galaxy, but one only survives being such an entity as long as all the particles remain in place, and when one particle was disrupted, I fell within a fantasy, eating the vermin of a lanky stranger.

I settled into this vision, a bouquet of decaying gravity that bent to the soft underbelly of a green ocean tide, which melted the moon, too soon, creating a tremendous shift—a disk formed under the weight of a displaced heaven, which caused the vision to transform into a trance, right when I became the headache of a serial killer, becoming the cause of the serial killing. First, the consistent pain. Second, the cannibal instinct. Third, the knife strokes. I then was assigned to be the motivation for an aroused understudy who learned of the

And the thing which he did displeased the LORD: wherefore he slew him also.

serial killer's killing methods while searching for himself, before evolving into the pen of a writer who wrote down his story, and then the ink that spelled the words, becoming them.

* * *

He carried me into his home when I arrived from towns away. He carried me across the threshold, telling me, "This is as close as we're getting to marriage," and then laughed a serious laugh, which was rich with the ignorance of me.

It was OK that he did not want to marry me, or that he did not believe in the philosophy of marriage—I only wanted to be joined in a holy covenant of him filling my brain with the discovery of all the hell everyone else in the world brought down upon him, and "they would pay somehow," he said.

I wanted to help. I wanted to remove his suffering, and so I told him I would do whatever it took to make him happy, and he looked me in the eyes and said, "You bring me down too. You are part of my suffering. You will end me this I know."

From that moment forward, he kept me beneath him, and I surrendered to his misogyny because I enjoyed defilement. I wanted him to defile me.

Tied to a bedpost were my limbs, all of them. Stretched out. The flesh surrounding the thin bones of my wrist 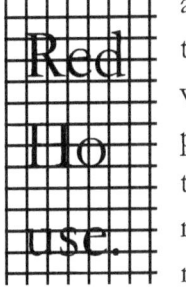 and ankles bled a delicious red wine that I found intoxicating. He wanted me to fight though, so I played along. I screamed until he thrust a dirty, wet dishtowel into my mouth. I fought, and he slapped me for several minutes until I was uncertain of my location. For two weeks, I  was a fixture on his bed, eating ice chunks to survive dehydration in between eating a baby blue dishrag.

The walls of my prison were cluttered with pictures of me, Polaroids taken from every angle, short and long. He tied up his carnal loose ends with those photos, never touching me in a purely sexual way.

I kept his headache intact. I was a throbbing vein that started as a vertical line down the middle of his forehead before veering off and going horizontal across the top of his eyebrow. That thick vein was intense, beating wildly, growing bigger, until he eventually removed it.

I stayed—strapped to that bed—until the odor of him caught the neighbor's attention. By then it was too late for me. I had already escaped into a production of a lizard pulling in a fly before becoming a human egg and roaming into a young girl who lived in suburbia.

A broken home kept me in a field that was part of the route to school. Ant piles filled the landscape, crowding the ground and ruining the vegetation. Once a year the ants sprung wings, and for a week, I ran through the field with millions of flying ants swarming around me. It was amazing. When the ants lost their wings and became earthbound once again, I still thought about those flying insects, praying for their return. Those ants took me away from the boring design of everything around me.

I sat around on most days and dreamed of my lover. I dreamed of a sinister animal. I found pleasure in his unruly world, in being with a dangerous person who everyone hated.

Dim. The light. Just right. A tortured flight. Into clouds that never release and always block the sun. To shun. The intent of hope. A slope. Into a bleached version of the residue that I always find, but never remove, so it becomes a part of everything around me. That residue oppresses my soul because I think about it obsessively, and now it cannot be cleaned away because there is too much of it. Even though no other soul knows about it, it leaves me guilt-ridden. It is blinding and beseeching. It fucks me up.

My lover was that bleached residue. My obsession. Where was he? Why was he hiding from me? When would I find him?

There he was many years later. Completely out of place. Drinking cheap liquor. Sinister. Barbaric. He hated the environment of his capitulation, so he claimed to be studying society from a barstool. Remember, he drips with molasses and has no poetic voice, although I give him one:

* * *

I went home trapped inside of his melaco mindscape. The luster in everything lost except in him.

Then I saw a rusty pipe in my peripheral vision as it came into my eyebrow—my eyes socket destroyed. The cold pavement of the

"Oh, this land tortures me. Sin at our steps and found in the hips and the whole of everything in this place. A sinful mingling of anguished eyes caught in antagonizing and embarrassing stares. Sexual urges with musical backing. Media droning, a subliminal drill into us. Who creates this base existence? Who controls the field of entertainment? Who are the players and the pawns? They are all the same, they are the devil's work."

alley was my bed as I was undressed for all my valuables. I lost my high heels, my purse, my fake pearl necklace, my mother's watch, the skin from my knees, and the feeling in all parts of my body. I hit the ground without any chance to brace myself. My chin hit

I caught the glimpse of three men, who provided the punctuation for everything my dream-lover was discussing.

Physically, I was never quite right after that mugging. It took several surgeries to find a way for my right eye to stay in its proper place because all of the bone around it was shattered. The eyesight in that one eye provided only a blurry and indistinct picture of my surroundings.

first and my head snapped back to an explosion of pain through my neck.

I was paralyzed for a time, seeing nothing but a blur, a rusty pipe and dark skin.

The indistinct images caused me to lose depth perception; everything appeared as two dimensional, and that is how I came to see the world. I learned nothing but regression from that point forward. The creativity in everything died.

* * *

You cannot create more energy. There is a certain amount of energy that is born in the world, but it never goes away. You cannot waste it. The population of the planet continues to grow, but it is not new energy being born; it comes from somewhere else. Something that is dying supplies the perceived life of something somewhere else. Something died so that you can live. The spontaneous explosion to life of a universe is a lie because that energy existed and died a slow painful death on a parallel plane.

We must always consider our enemies. We cannot pretend that the enemy does not exist. Forget finding common ground.

Existence? Sure. Existence is alive, but it is our foe, as we continue to build existence— killing—into everything we see.

I arrive in the present.

I am still two-dimensional, and so is everything around me.

My pale skin is the whitest it has ever been. I mean white, like the pages of my journal. Pure skin, blue veins. Heavy blue, an intricate system of wires that guide ashen skin. Nothing reflects its surface color anymore. Sacred. Undiluted. I see authority. I see honor. In ivory. So I surrender to it—

I am breathing into a machine and seeping into me—an intravenous drip—is crystalloids, an aqueous solution of mineral salts is an iron fist. My kidneys hurt. My skin hurts. It is the first pain that I have felt outside of emotion since my accident.

I look over to flowers of white with white thorns on white stems in white liquid. There is no vase, it appears. The water and the flowers float in the air.

A white knight arrives. I do not understand the words he delivers—hijacked from a revolution. However, he conveys his message in a way that I find eloquent, so I take the words, misplace them, and conceal their meaning within the primer underneath my hide.

"No one among us has any conception of the dimensions of shame that will befall us when our black veil is removed to reveal our loathsome crime, a crime that outweighs every other offense and narcissistically distorts the infinite meaning of life."

Then the black came upon us in hot waves. We fought the darkness the best we could.

I am in love.

I shoot him. A right of passage. Imagine it. The system is alive. Here is the story:

I sit in a room and say, "I'll do it."

Initially, the men are offended. Send a woman to do a man's job? Molasses stands, flows to me, and looks down upon me. I close my eyes and wait for a lashing while I say, "I love you, baby. I didn't mean to intrude."

He braces himself, trying to keep his fists to his sides. He shakes with restraint.

I take a ride with the men. It is a quiet trip as we all gather our thoughts. Orange radiance spills away from the horizon to other continents. The wind of the chilly night enters the

The streets are purple; everything rides on the edge of purple, in two dimensions.

Everything is rounded with a blunt tip.

car windows, filling our sail, riding with us. There is a gun in my hand. It is solid and warm. We drive through the inner city. Ramshackle buildings are attached to bloodstained sidewalks. The buildings pull hard into the hazy sky, attempting to escape.

I see the line of another universe on top of mine. There **I see depth.** is pleasure in the many colors of the new offering, but there is still immense agony in its world. Edifices collide. Lights spar in three dimensions. *Its shirt is off, its ribs is are waves.* The streets wrap around me in despair. A spirit sitting next to me is crying. I reach for it, but it cannot feel me, see me. It is in a hotel room, a phone is ringing against its ear. It longs for an answer.

There is a drip of ten billion years. It creates a hole, one hundred miles deep, but the opening is as big around as a dime. I wait until a flame

I wait until a flame melts me and then I pour inside.

melts me and then I pour inside the orifice. The bottom of the hole connects to a cavern. I spot a shallow grave and another, and a thousand more, some so shallow that the ridges and curves of bones protrude. There was haste in their disposal. As I walk further into the cavern, it is impossible to avoid stepping on bones, and in some cases, complete carcasses, thinly decomposed and leaving bloodstains on the carpet of black mold. The ceiling drips caramelized sugar. There is a beast ahead to my center.

"Shoot me please," it taunts. I look down to see the gun still in my hand, still warm from my heated skin. This beast is gorgeous. His mind expands before me, rearranging itself in a continuous flow of new  color and design, floating above me in a magnificent arrangement of bedazzling lights.

* * *

Someone who I loved a great deal thought that I could not write about those things in which I did not experience. I told him that there was zero truth to it. At the time, I was a writer, and I wrote quite a bit. I told him that just because a writer can empathize, does not mean they must live the literal life of the fictional characters in their stories. But I was wrong. Empathy comes from an experience, but it does not have to broadcast from its current form. My lives have been both alive and not alive, but always energetic. I may have been a flame or a thought or a death wish or a blot of ink or a king. I may have been a broken woman in love with a molasses man without a refined bone, who was pulled from her shackles by the kiss of a another man, who others claimed was my enemy. To some, that kiss may have only been an arbitrary peck across the broad lips of a dying man, but it meant much more to the overlords. It was a kiss that showed enlightenment.

* * *

I am pulled away from the moribund man and shattered to pieces by my lanky lover and all the people who love him, and then I am sent into the sky by way of a burning effigy to my own son. I do not stop ascending until I reach nirvana, where I am given godly properties.

My empathy, which formed through my many experiences, became the basis for the creation of a failed utopia that orbits a G2 star along with several other celestial bodies, and is located within the spiral arm of an SBbc galaxy, about eight kiloparsecs from the galaxy's center.

I had not interest in sitting through a billion years of chemicals and dissolve to get to higher life forms.

The successful dystopia took on the many forms of my exploits, and today I sit above it all and watch my world destroy itself because it has no other choice.

I created life in my own image so it was bound

Instead I implanted the base of their arrival in sequenced stages. Science is fiction.

to fail, but it is still a shame that in the

The flaw is within me.

end, lives of higher intelligence would take energy and destroy with it. It is all that my creations do, though.

I often find myself entering singular minds and drifting through their thoughts And there is nothing that can be done about it. in an attempt to find something that I did not know, but I never learn anything— deconstruction occurs at all outposts.

I have given up hope in everything.

We will die together. Their failed God, my failed planet.

JANUARY 23, 2012

The baby had to go.

JANUARY 24, 2012

And my one-day cloud of twenty-five consecutive days began:

The ghastly nights turned to days and then again. And all over. Every second revealed itself as an itch. There was no form of entertainment except a Shakespearian tragedy and a race to suicide. The television never turned on, the blinds never opened themselves, the bed never rolled out from beneath a sheet and comforter. The lights never stabbed the darkness. I occupied a corner of the room with the telephone beside me on the floor, calling, a continuous call to an empty red house.

The carpet of the hotel was crunchy and some shade of brown; it was hard to tell without any light. The floor might as well have been concrete; it was hard, refusing to forgive. I pissed myself on that floor. I shat myself and sat in it. I rotted away.

A maid came in the room to clean one day, and I screamed her into a retreat; she did not return. Then the hallucinations began, somewhere in the middle of twenty-five days—one day—of no sleep and no sustenance, including water— believe it—I fell into a trance of the ringing of a phone that no one ever answered.

The ring became a bridge over a river that was stagnant. Dead fish floated and dissolved into distorted bends of light. I jumped off the bridge and into a bed of sludge. I landed and then sank. Everything was dying.

I recalled dead babies. Several.

I had exiled myself while I waited for a black heart to give me an order—

I would die slowly because I do not believe that sudden death is the answer; it must be plodding. It must be done through clean and honest humility. It must include the proper packaging. There must be anguish without clemency. Poison is not a sharp knife. Poison is to rearrange body chemicals into a new formula.

I could not even cry. My eyes were dry. My tongue was a ridge without moisture. I was like this for days.

Then people occupied my room. The sun shined through a fast-drawn curtain. I was blinded, gripping the phone's receiver and refusing to release it. I finally heard a "hello" from the phone as men in white uniforms put me on a stretcher. The phone snapped from my hand and hit the wall as they carried me away. I heard, "hello, hello, who is this?" I attempted to make a sound and there was nothing but a shallow moan that no one heard. Twenty-five days—one day.

We are not free. There is no free will. No soul anywhere can make a resolution without an opposite force eventually tearing it away.

Existence. Our enemy.

The *lovehatelove* saga continues for free on May 1, 2012, at:

http://robinmichaelsmith.com/lhl.html
Password: ChristinaTheAstonishing